QUARTET ENCOUNTERS

THE GAMES OF NIGHT

Much of Stig Dagerman's best writing is to be found in his short stories. The present volume presents a selection of the most interesting of them, as well as an unusually sensitive autobiographical piece, 'A Child's Memoirs'. His work is original and daring. A critic has written of him: 'Everything was briefer, swifter, more fiery and more sharply felt for him than for other people. His books exploded from him.'

STIG DAGERMAN

Stig Dagerman was regarded as the most talented young writer of the Swedish post-war generation. By the time he was twenty-six he had published four novels, a collection of short stories, a book of travel sketches and four full-length plays – an astonishing output which was brought to a tragic end by his death in 1954.

Jack O'Connell
Seattle
4 May 1996

STIG DAGERMAN

The
Games of Night

Translated from the Swedish by
NAOMI WALFORD
With an Introduction by
MICHAEL MEYER

Quartet Books   London Melbourne New York

Published by Quartet Books Limited 1986
A member of the Namara Group
27/29 Goodge Street, London W1P 1FD

Originally published in Stockholm as *Nattens Lekar*
and *Vårt Behov Av Tröst*.

British Library Cataloguing in Publication Data

Dagerman, Stig
The games of night.
I. Title
839.7'374[F]   PT9875.D12

ISBN 0-7043-0024-9

Reproduced, printed and bound in Great Britain
by Nene Litho and Woolnough Bookbinding
both of Wellingborough, Northants

Contents

An Introduction

I FIRST saw Stig Dagerman in 1948, when he came to speak in a debate at Uppsala University. He was then 25 years old and already had three novels, three plays, a book of travel reportage and a collection of short stories to his credit. He was above medium height and well built, with a gentle, broad-boned face. What one noticed about him first was his eyes, which were large and—I had almost said staring, but that word would give an entirely wrong impression; they were intensely reflective, mild and unseeing, like the eyes of a blind man. He spoke haltingly, in a low and scarcely audible voice, and my recollection is that his line of argument was rather muddled, but that out of it emerged several sharply perceived truths.

Another five years passed before I actually met him, in the early summer of 1953, at a small party given by his publisher, Ragnar Svanström, at the latter's country cottage on an island in the Stockholm archipelago. Dagerman was there with Anita Björk, the lovely and talented young actress whom he was shortly to marry; eight of us ate by candlelight, and then he and I walked and talked on the shore outside. I found him, in his shy way, a delightfully gay and impulsive companion. We spoke in English, for he talked the language well—his French and German were also good—and, like so many Swedes, he enjoyed conversing in a foreign tongue. When we returned to Stockholm later that evening, I drove him and Anita Björk back to their house at Enebyberg, just north of Stockholm. We continued talking late into the night, and finally I was put to bed in their guest room.

During the next three months, I visited them often, and the

7

pattern was always the same. The three of us (for we were usually alone) would talk until about one o'clock. Then Anita would yawn, and go to bed; whereupon there would be a change of subject. Up to now we had talked about the theatre, literature, people, the state of the world—all the subjects which people aged thirty like to discuss on summer nights— but once Stig and I were alone the conversation almost invariably turned to football, for which he had an extraordinary passion. Late summer is the beginning of the football season in Sweden and we would discuss the prospects of this team and that until it struck two and I would totter upstairs to my guest room. Even then he did not always go to bed. Sometimes he would climb the extra flight to his study in a small tower which rose above the house, and I would fall asleep to the sound of his typewriter.

This typewriter, alas, now held a very different significance for him from what it had symbolised when I had first seen him in 1948. Then, he had been a prolific young author at the height of his powers; but after 1949, a strange kind of paralysis had overcome him. Every author's nightmare of finding himself unable to write had, for Stig Dagerman, become reality, and for the past three and a half years he had produced nothing. It was not that he was short of ideas; he would conceive an exciting plan for a book or a play, and would ring his publisher in an ecstacy of excitement; an advance would be paid; but somehow he, who had formerly been able to write 60 pages in a single night, could now scarcely complete a chapter. The tappings of the typewriter which penetrated from his room in the tower to my small guest room below were the efforts of a man to overcome a paralysis; a paralysis from which he was never able to escape, and which a year later was to drive him to suicide.

8

One evening that August, Anita Björk telephoned me and invited me to a wedding. 'Whose?' I asked, and she replied: 'Ours'. Although they were, and had for several years been deeply in love, both distrusted the idea of marriage; but now, one sunny afternoon, I found myself standing in a small room in the local parsonage and watched Anita Björk become Stig Dagerman's wife. We went to a lovely sixteenth-century inn by the side of a lake for dinner, and then, as is the Swedish manner, returned after the shortest of intervals to Enebyberg for supper. It was almost the last time I saw Stig Dagerman, for shortly afterwards I returned to England, and sixteen months later, in November, 1954, he gassed himself in the garage of the house at Enebyberg.

Stig Dagerman was born on October 25th, 1923, in a small farmhouse outside the village of Älvkarleby, about a hundred miles north of Stockholm. He was the illegitimate son of a quarryman called Helmer Jansson and a telephone operator named Helga Andersson; she came from Härnosand in the far north of Sweden to the farmhouse, which was the home of Helmer Jansson's parents, to have her child. Olof Lagercrantz, Dagerman's biographer, has described his entrance into the world:

'At 11.30 in the night, she gave birth to a boy. It was a rainy night in the middle of the potato harvest, and everyone was tired. There was no telephone, and when the pains began a daughter of the house, aged sixteen, saddled one of the two horses and rode through the rain to the village to fetch the midwife. . . . The mother stayed at the farm for two months. . . .'

And Dagerman himself, basing his picture on what his grandparents must have told him, describes his mother's departure:

9

'On New Year's Day she went to the station with a small bag in one hand. She said nothing, but simply walked out of their lives. The snow whirled the old year away. She never came back.'

She believed she would shortly marry Helmer Jansson and could then take the boy to live with her. But the parents quarrelled and parted company, and Stig Dagerman remained with his grandparents at the farm near Älvkarleby. They took care of him until he was eleven; during that time, he saw his father seldom and his mother never. But he was devoted to his grandparents, and his childhood was happy; it was the only period of his life which was. He has described it vividly in the autobiographical fragment which appears in this volume, *A Child's Memoirs*:

'Grandfather and grandmother were in their way the finest people I have ever met. They were not the kind by whom one is carved, finely, accurately and precisely. By them one was rough-hewn, as a hedge-stake is shaped, or a board for a loose-box. They did not like people who were fretwork; they wanted one to serve a useful purpose, if only as a hedge-stake. All their days they had to toil like oxen, round and round without stopping, for their very lives.'

People who knew Dagerman as a child speak of him as having been lively and cheerful. He loved to listen to the tramps who used to visit the farm; for his grandmother had a soft heart, and was known never to turn a tramp from her door. She and her husband were deeply religious people; each evening, they read aloud from the Bible, and these Bible readings, the tales of the tramps, and the reminiscences and story-telling of his grandparents were Stig Dagerman's early education, far more than the lessons he learned at the village school.

But when he was twelve, his father, Helmer Jansson, married a wife (not Stig's mother), and Stig went to live with him in Stockholm. Helmer Jansson was still a quarryman, and the world into which Stig now entered was very different from that of his grandparents. It was a world of working-class people trying to become bourgeois, farmers being slowly transformed into townsmen—'women who still, after ten years in the city, fumbled awkwardly with the taps on the gas-stove, and whose main preoccupation in life was a fixed determination that they should not be forced, as their mothers had been, to wear themselves out prematurely by heavy labour and incessant childbearing.' Dagerman, in his writings, continually contrasts the farming world of his grandparents with the equally poor, but less free life of his parents in Stockholm. He was, throughout his life, like so many Swedes of his generation, a countryman trying uneasily to adapt himself to town life, and he never succeeded; for him, happiness ended when he left his grandparents' farm.

When he was 16, his grandfather was murdered by a madman, and his grandmother died a few weeks later from the shock.

'The evening I heard about the murder, I went to the City Library and tried to write a poem to the dead man's memory. Nothing came of it but a few pitiful lines which I tore up in shame. But out of that shame, out of that impotence and grief, something was born—something which I believe was the desire to become a writer; that is to say, to be able to tell of what it is to mourn, to have been loved, to be left lonely. . . .'

The years that followed were indeed lonely; he has told how he used to go down to the railway station to be among people, and would stand there until he was turned out. 'I dreamed of standing there one day with a ticket to China in my pocket, which I would show when the police came. But I never had a ticket to China. I went on writing, and the same thought lay behind that. A little later I heard the International sung at a meeting—not for the first time; but it was the first time it had made such an impression on me. It was like a violent conversion. I became a syndicalist, and slowly I grew aware of the hard, strife-filled happiness of infusing new vigour into an empty faith. . . . I became editor of a revolutionary, antifascist youth newspaper. . . .'

When he was 20, Dagerman married Anne Marie Götze, an 18-year-old German refugee whose parents had both fought, and been imprisoned, in the Spanish Civil War. Dagerman and his young wife were too poor to afford a place of their own, and lived in the kitchen alcove of her parents' one-room flat. Olof Lagencrantz describes the effect that this new life had on Dagerman.

'He lived with refugees, and became himself a refugee. He learned, in the Götzes' kitchen, to look with distaste on the security and smugness which characterised Swedish everyday life. In this home he seemed to hear the heart of Europe beat, met other refugees, tramps of a new kind who had been driven on to the roads not, as in his grandmother's time, by lack of work, but by lack of the right belief.'

Lagercrantz adds that, by mixing with the Götzes and their refugee friends, Dagerman succeeded in identifying himself with his generation in combatant Europe, and that he found thereby something of the calm which he had known on his grandparents' farm.

The year after his marriage, in 1944, Dagerman became cultural editor of the syndicalist newspaper *Arbetaren*, and came into contact with the group of young writers called *fyrtiotalisterna* (writers of the forties) who were then beginning to make their presence felt in Sweden. A young Swedish critic, Sven-Arne Bergman, has written of this group:

'To the young Swedish writers, the forties brought the collapse of many beautiful myths and alluring 'isms' which the previous decade had greedily embraced. The literary climate veered towards pessimism, towards themes of darkness and destruction, and suddenly a new and bitter awareness developed. The European modernism of the twenties had had only mild repercussions in Sweden; now experimental modernism became the order of the day. The new poets took the lead, but prose writing soon followed suit. . . . Dagerman was on the editorial committee of 40-tal, the short-lived but influential magazine which launched the new ideas . . . (and) he has come to stand out almost as the incarnation of that tortured period, a symbolic figure whose death seemed to confirm the conception of the poet as the martyr to his vision.'

The influence of these politically conscious young writers, of whom the most notable was the poet Erik Lindegren, combined with the influence of the Götzes and their circle to liberate Dagerman's creative talent, and during the next five years he poured out novels, plays, short stories and poems with extraordinary prolificity and intensity. In 1945, when he was 22, he wrote his first novel, *The Snake*. In the next year, a second novel followed, *The Island of the Damned*; and in 1947 he produced *The Games of Night* (a collection of short stories, from which most of the stories which make up the present volume are taken), a book of reportage from post-war Germany entitled *German Autumn*, and his first play, *The Man Condemned to Death*. This last was excitingly produced at the Royal Theatre in Stockholm by Alf Sjöberg, the director of the films *Frenzy* and *Miss Julie*, and was a brilliant success. In 1948, he wrote two more plays, *The Shadow of*

13

Mart and *The Upstart*, and a third novel, *Burnt Child*; and in 1949, a fourth novel, *Wedding Troubles*, and a fourth play, *No-one Goes Free* (a dramatisation of *Burnt Child*).

Thus, at the age of 26, he found himself the author of four novels, four plays, a book of short stories and a book of reportage, as well as numerous poems and articles contributed to newspapers and magazines. Except for *No-one Goes Free*, which he disliked and never published, Dagerman's work during this period varied remarkably little in quality, and he was already being spoken of, not without justification, as the most promising young dramatist-novelist to have emerged in Sweden since Pär Lagerkvist.

But then this strange paralysis to which reference has already been made overcame him. The desire to write remained strong, and he planned numerous works—a novel with a Paris setting, another called *The Tiger Heart*, a third called *The Snowflake*, a fourth which was to be a vision of the future in the Orwell manner, a fifth which was to have been quasi-autobiographical, a sixth based on the life of the nineteenth-century poet Almqvist; but he, who had once been so prolific, now found himself unable to complete anything more than isolated chapters. He made a journey to Australia to write a film for Svensk Filmindustri, returning to Europe across America, but even this could not shake off the spell under which he laboured; the film was never written.

More than once he tried to take his life, once by means of a razor blade, several times by remaining in a closed garage and letting the engine of his car run. In 1951 he wrote to Anita Björk, whom he had recently met and fallen in love with:

'It is a terrible expérience, which I know you will be spared, to feel oneself disintegrate and sink, when one is praying to be allowed to grow and to climb. Now that the choice has finally come between living like a pariah and dying wretchedly, I must choose as I have done, because I believe that a bad person's death makes the world a better place. God grant that our child may be like you. I have loved you, and will do so for as long as I am allowed to. Forgive me, but please believe me. Stig.'

The letter was never sent, and was found torn into small pieces.

Anita Björk and Stig Dagerman were deeply and mutually in love; and whenever I saw him, during the summer of 1953, he seemed calm and content. But he was, though I did not realise it, suffering from schizophrenia, and he had dark moods, which I never saw; often he felt an overpowering urge to be alone, and would get out of bed in the middle of the night, take the car from the garage and drive for hours into the night, as though he longed to enter the darkness and be swallowed up in it.

On the morning of November 4th, 1954, he was found in the garage at the wheel of his car. The garage was full of gas; the engine was turned off, but this time he had lacked the strength to leave the car, and he was dead.

The stories translated here reveal Dagerman's various facets as a writer. *A Child's Memoirs* and *Sleet* show him as a portrayer of country people. *Where's My Iceland Jersey?* and *Open the Door, Richard* reveal people swinging uneasily between the primitive instincts of the countryman and the bourgeois way of life to which they are trying to adapt themselves. *A Thousand Years with the Lord* (a chapter from the projected novel about the poet Almqvist) shows Dagerman in his favourite no-man's-land where reality and fantasy merge. Reality and fantasy, the world of the countryman and the world of the city—Dagerman was never fully able to reconcile them; although he wanted to be the conscience of the world, his world was in fact a small private one, and it was the inability to break through its walls that drove him to creative paralysis and, ultimately, death. Yet, like his masters Strindberg and Kafka, he photographed his small, split world with a vivid and faithful clarity, and sometimes one is haunted by a secret and uneasy suspicion that his private vision, like Strindberg's and Kafka's, may in fact be nearer the truth of things than those visions of the great humanists, such as Tolstoy and Balzac, which people call universal.

MICHAEL MEYER

A
CHILD'S
MEMOIRS

A Child's Memoirs

CREATIVE imagination awakens early. As children we are all 'makers'. Later, as a rule, we're broken of the habit; so the art of being a creative writer consists, among other things, in not allowing life or people or money to turn us aside from it.

I took to 'making things up' very early. Reality—though that is far too grand a word—became warmer, more amusing, more fun to look at if one rearranged it a little. Not much. It was in an old farm standing high above a broad, swift river. Springs ran under the house, so it was always cold and draughty. The farm stood by itself in a big enclosure, and of the first years I remember only the winters, when the wind came howling in and covered the whole world with snow. Drifts rose above the windows and one hardly ever went out. Merely to visit the slop pail that stood in the entrance lobby, where snow whirled in under the door like letters, was an adventure. The house was full of aunts and uncles and cats. The grown-ups were always bickering. The cats mewed. I used to crouch like a cat in the warmth of the fire, and an older cousin whom I greatly admired could sit in bed a good way off and spit accurately on my foot. One morning in winter, when as usual I had stayed in bed late because I was considered delicate and perhaps was, there was a miaowing and squealing under the blanket. When I lifted it the bed was full of kittens. The cat had littered beside me while I slept.

Sometimes in those winters it was Christmas. Once grandfather gave me a bow and arrows with padded points, so that I could shoot indoors. At other Christmases there were little bears or toy cars that one could wind up. They came from Stockholm and from father whom I had never seen and always made up stories about. But one summer when he came I thought he looked like all the other Stockholmers who used to look in on us because we had such a beautiful view. They used the word 'also' and wrinkled their noses at the smell indoors and because we all drank from the same dipper. When they had gone we laughed at them in an embarrassed sort of way, and not for long, as at something not quite normal.

2

Between the long winters came short summers. In memory they are always very hot. The grass by the house turns yellow and when one runs sand whirls up from the ground. Drought and crop failure. Drooping grain and smoking fields. The river dwindles and new islands of sand and mud rise from the water like menacing shadows of hunger. The grown-ups look at the sky, but there are only thick cirrus clouds to be seen, and straight yellow smoke on the horizon from the Skutskär works. One day the Meeting House caught fire and the road was filled with running, pointing people. A big yellow cloud with mourning edges rose over the community. We stayed at home on the farm and smelt the smoke, but were too proud to run down there. We were yeoman farmers.

The nights with the two old people were stifling and oppressive. Nobody in the whole house slept. Someone would get up and clatter the water-dipper in the kitchen. There was never a breath of air or coolness, and the windows were left open all night. Sometimes the horses had dreams and kicked in their stalls: a muffled, frightening sound. Perhaps some tramp might be lurking, matches in hand, behind the straw stacks. Nothing was so greatly dreaded as fire. The old man would pad out in his underpants and come back presently with the cat. Then early in the morning the guns began. This was a noise on the horizon from the training ground more than six miles away, and it hung over these hot summers like a big, black shadow. There they go—and again. . . . God grant we don't have war. It was only sometimes, when the woods round the ground had been set alight and smoke billowed up on the skyline, that the guns fell silent for a while.

Heat and despair. But the Stockholmers who lodged up in the village came down to the farm and set up croquet-hoops in our grassy yard. The days echoed with the crack of mallets and gunfire and towndwellers' laughter. It was difficult to understand, but gradually one began to hate the people who played croquet and laughed and bathed while the grain was burning down, while cows lowed for water and somebody had seen a snake nearer the house than in any previous year. In the evenings they always left a hoop or two behind, and when any of us caught his clog in it in the twilight he kicked both hoop and clog high up towards the moon, in relieving rage.

The moon. Sometimes, when it was full—this must have been in August—the butcher's boy bicycled with me on the cross-bar to a little village on the hill. Behind him he carried fresh red meat in a margarine box. We stopped outside the gates and tinkled our bell, and old men and women came out of the houses, took the meat from the box, squeezed it, nipped it, and tossed it back. Sometimes they put a pinch of snuff under their upper lips before going further through our stock. But when we rode back down the hill the box was always empty.

One morning I did something dreadful. It was not only the croquet players I hated, and the soldiers who carried on their manoeuvres over our land, trampling down the grain, riding their panting horses along all the smoking roads and haunting the river in their queer boats. (One evening when we were sitting on the bank watching them, a captain fell into the lake. We didn't laugh, but we felt that at last we had been done some sort of justice.) No, above all I hated the sun, and one morning when the grass glowed and not a cloud was to be seen either in the Gävle sky or in the Uppsala sky, I threw myself on my knees in the shade of the lilac hedge and cursed the sun, and prayed God and all other powers to put it out.

It was the first time I had ever prayed, and afterwards I was exhausted and afraid. For several nights I couldn't sleep, being convinced that so burning a prayer must be fulfilled. But the sun rose every morning to scorch the potato-tops and the rye and the Stockholmers. I sat down by the gate and watched the women bicycling past in their colourful frocks. Bicycling past. . . . But I knew that some day one of them would put on her brakes, jump off opposite the gate and lift me up. It would be my mother, whom I had never seen. They talked about her sometimes, and how she came to the farm and bore me one night in the middle of the potato-lifting (when there's so much to do as it is!) and vanished after a fortnight. She used to wash herself all over in hot water every night: that was the memorable thing about her.

Some summers she was going to arrive on a bicycle. Afterwards it was always a car: one of those high, black ones like a top hat, with a shade over the windscreen looking like eyebrows. But whenever a car did stop it brought only an agent for sewing-machines or flypapers or oil-engines. Everybody else in the world had parents: I had only grandparents.

Grandfather and grandmother were in their way the finest people I have ever met. They were not the kind by whom one is carved, finely, accurately and precisely. By them one was rough-hewn, as a hedge-stake is shaped, or a board for a loose-box. They did not like people who were fretwork; they wanted one to serve a useful purpose, if only as a hedge-stake. All their days they had had to toil like oxen, round and round without stopping, for their very lives. They never gave up hope, but they despised idleness as the chief of the deadly sins. Next to it came pernicketyness, polished insincere manners, pettiness and arrogance. They had many faults themselves, but never hid them. They could not and would not hide them.

I didn't know them until they were old. Their childhood, youth and middle age I know of only through what I was told, by them and others. Grandfather came from a farm in south Roslagen. He was one of a large family; he lost his father early and the work was hard. As a boy in the '70s he drove hay to the haymarket in Stockholm. He had to drive at night so as to arrive early in the morning, and he used always to sleep on the way, to be awake when he got there. One night he woke up in the ditch with the load on top of him. The only thing he could remember of his journeys to town was that one night in 1878 the load overturned. The town itself made no impression on him. There were too many people, too little seriousness, too much 'clatter'.

When still young he had to leave home. He might have emigrated, but did not. Always he had a love or rather a passion for the soil that kept his life in equilibrium. He worked as farmhand under ill-natured, miserly Uppland peasants, he helped to build Älvkarleby power station, and landed at last in the Skutskär works. That was in the time when men toiled at least fourteen hours a day, and the foremen would send them inside the drums through which the sawdust was blown out from the saws. Half-suffocated and blinded by the whirling particles, they crawled about in the darkness, digging out a free passage for the sawdust. He made the nine-mile journey home to his family every fortnight. There was of course no money for a bicycle, and he had to walk like everyone else. The men lived in shacks in the factory area—shacks so full of cockroaches that the food had to be kept in an office safe.

The thing that helped him to endure it cannot have been necessity alone, but rather the craving for land that beset him all his life. He was fifty-six when at last he satisfied that craving. He bought a ruinous old holding whose soil was too full of stones to plough; the stones had to be dug out, but as he couldn't afford spades he made do with mattocks. He was not just a hard worker—he was a furious one. He used to take me out into the fields with him, sit me on the bank of a ditch and let me watch him. Long afterwards, when he had set everything in order, he used to point with his whip whenever we drove past the churchyard. It was the stone wall he pointed at. In that lay all the stones he had cleared from his fields, and he used to say that he was glad that one day he would lie beside his own stones. It was not sentimentality or vanity. It was exultation over good work done.

The first years, which were my first years too, were not good. It was not so much the malicious backbiting and the mean tricks—always the lot of a proud newcomer—but the poverty that tripped him up. It was the valuable new horse, uninsured, which tried to jump a fence and impaled itself on a stake. It was the young son who drowned the day he came home from his mother's funeral. Above all it was the interest and the mortgages. 'Interest' was one of the first words I learned, and I know that when a house is mortgaged to the roof-ridge it's not just a phrase but a real weight, which lies on the shoulders like a yoke.

But although the sulphite works had broken him and rheumatism was beginning to rend him to pieces, he would not be beaten. When things were at their worst he broke into the woods and cleared and cultivated single-handed an acre of good soil, won from stones, moss and mixed woodland. I remember the dreadful green business-letters arriving, and how sometimes he couldn't rest even at night, but would get up and walk out into the dark fields with his seedbag, and sow; or harness the horses and take harrow or plough out in the middle of the night. From a safe distance people shook their heads or laughed. Afterwards I used to think he must have been like a poet at that time, mastering intractable material, conscious perhaps that in itself it was of little use, but nevertheless necessary, for the sake of the work, for the sake of the poem.

The rheumatism won. He began groaning at night, and in the daytime he could hardly get out of bed. Sometimes when the fit seized him he went out to the stables, but he couldn't even get the harness down off the hook; he would go in again then, lock his door, lie on his bed and weep. Thus in time he grew bitter and suspicious. He remembered the early years, and fancied that people wanted to take advantage of his helplessness and throw him off the farm. Sometimes he wouldn't allow strangers into the house at all. With the whole force of his obstinacy he was convinced that people wished him ill and that the place was going to rack and ruin now that he could no longer see to things himself. He was ashamed of being unable to work, and sometimes the shame turned to hatred. Every August we had to take an ear of rye to him, in his room. We had to put the grains in his mouth, and he bit them to see if they were ripe. No reaping could start until he had convinced himself that the time had come. I don't know what he did after they shut the door on him, but to me his face seemed to show that this was one of his happiest hours, and one of his hardest.

Grandmother was a tremendous worker and she complemented him by her gentleness. She was the daughter of a poor fisherman in the same parish. She had had altogether six weeks schooling with the parish clerk, during which time she learned to enumerate the United States of America. Right up to her death she could recite all forty-eight of them by heart. Of her earlier life I know only that she had many children and that several of them died young. What I remember about her was her capacity for kindness and for helping people. Although we were probably the poorest of all the poor peasants in that parish it would never have entered her head to turn a tramp from the door. In the end the other farmers got into the habit of sending all the tramps over to us. During the worst years of the depression we might have three or four in one evening, and throughout my childhood moves a procession of beggars: ragged old men who halted with bent heads inside the door, others who talked and told stories which only they themselves laughed at, hollowly, between coughs; others that were daft and had to surrender their matches at night, and bitter youngsters who talked loud and heatedly about the shots in Ådalen.* Grandmother looked after them all, not officiously or sentimentally, but rather as if

*The reference is to a clash between demonstrating workers and military in 1931, when five workers were killed.

26

it were natural that those very people should come—as if they were expected and had their places at the table reserved for them.

Not only tramps came. The first types of humanity I learned to recognise were the horse-copers and gipsies: they sent the women and children in while they themselves stayed out on the cart or sleigh, and the eyes of the women and children always wandered over the walls as if they were looking for silver or gold. The children were thin and bold, and when the women came into the warm and found that nobody threw them out, they made themselves at home by the fire and suckled their babies there without embarrassment. When the gipsies came through the village all the children had to hide their toys, but after I had seen a little girl kneel by the pig-bucket in the cowshed porch and guzzle up the swill like a calf, I did so no longer.

Grandmother always had a chunk of rye bread for anyone who was hungry, and she would slip the horse-coper's own beast a wisp of hay, stealthily, so that grandfather—who hated horse-dealers and all who ill-treated animals—should not see. When the officers rode by along the road she would sometimes go out and stand in the way, to scold them for riding their horses to death. One winter a fellow from Dalarna came who could play the fiddle, and he was allowed to stay for two years because he played so well. She had that rare quality: the courage to show love; and when I grew a little older and more understanding, she gave me a staggering sense of how great a quality generosity can be, when it is neither hypocritical, sentimental nor self-centred.

Grandfather fell victim to a senseless act of violence. There was a local man who had some kind of obsession, and one evening he lay in wait in the lilac hedge, with a knife.

27

Grandfather went out to the paddock to see to the horses for the night. It was already dark, and after a while he was heard to cry out. When his people found him he was lying on his back in the grass. They helped him up and he told them that somebody had knifed him and then disappeared over the fence. The absurd thing was that no one believed him. They supposed that he had been kicked by a horse, and tried to persuade him of this while they helped him back towards the house. Then for the last time in his life he got angry and demanded to walk by himself, since nobody would believe him; and in the darkness, alone with his obstinacy and his seventeen knife-wounds, he walked as far as the gate. There he fell, and a few minutes later he was dead. Grandmother died some weeks later from the shock.

When this happened I was no longer there. I was at college in Stockholm, and I thought I should never be able to bear the loss of those from whom I had learnt most, and whom I most loved. The evening I heard about the murder I went to the City Library and tried to write a poem to the dead man's memory. Nothing came of it but a few pitiful lines which I tore up in shame. But out of that shame, out of that impotence and grief, something was born—something which I believe was the desire to become a writer: that is to say to be able to tell of what it is to mourn, to have been loved, to be left lonely.

4

After that something new began. I had always felt alone. The farmers' children regarded me as a Stockholm boy, an intruder, although I tried to learn all their bad words as quickly as I could, to please them. In Stockholm I was the clodhopping yokel, whose short overcoat was laughed at for a whole term. Now I was forsaken indeed. It was the autumn that the steamer *Ragvald* sank by the City Hall, and every evening I went down to Central Station and stood there in the milling crowds until I was chased out. I dreamed a dream of standing there one day with a ticket to China in my pocket, which I would show when the police came. But I never had a ticket to China. I went on writing, and the same thought lay behind that. A little later I heard the International sung at a meeting—not for the first time; but it was the first time it had made such an impression on me. It was like a violent conversion. I became a syndicalist, and slowly I grew aware of the hard, strife-filled happiness of infusing new vigour into an empty faith. During that struggle it became clear to me too how much help I should have from authorship, not as an end but as a means. I became editor of a revolutionary, anti-fascist youth newspaper, had the first number confiscated and was inordinately proud of the fact that it sometimes took the police three weeks to read through my (schoolboy) mail.

On Saturdays and Sundays throughout nearly all my schooldays I turned paper-boy. On Saturday afternoons I ran down to my boat with my Latin grammar in my pocket, revelling in not having to be a schoolboy. This was partly pride, of course, but also a longing to come really close to the people who had meant most to me: the poorest peasants and the poorest labourers. The same urge made me a bus-conductor when I was in the top form but one, though at first I was so bus-sick that I had to get out and vomit at the end stations.

As a newspaper-boy I learned once more to dislike arrogance and later to dislike bad weeklies. Once I sent poems to *Hela Världen*, but they were never printed. Nor were they returned. In school competitions I had better luck, and in my graduation year I won a week's holiday in the mountains, with a short story. But that trip ended in tragedy: I lost a very good friend and room-mate in an avalanche. When I came back I knew beyond all doubt what I must be. I must be a writer. And I knew what I must write: the book of my dead.

THE
GAMES
OF
NIGHT

The Games of Night

SOMETIMES at night, when his mother was crying in the bedroom and only unknown steps clattered on the stairs, Åke had a game which he played instead of crying. He pretended that he was invisible and that he could wish himself anywhere, just by thinking it. On those evenings there was only one place to wish oneself, and so Åke was suddenly there. He never knew how he had arrived; he just knew that he was standing in a room. What it looked like he didn't know, because he hadn't the right eyes for it, but it was full of the smoke of cigarettes and pipes, and people laughed suddenly, frighteningly, for no reason, and women who couldn't talk clearly leaned across a table and laughed in just the same, dreadful way. It cut through Åke like knives, yet he was glad to be there. On the table around which everybody was sitting were a number of bottles, and as soon as a glass was empty a hand unscrewed the screw-stopper and filled it again.

Åke who was invisible lay down on the floor and crawled under the table without anybody who sat there noticing him. In his hand he carried an invisible drill and without a moment's hesitation he set the point of it against the underside of the table-top and started drilling upwards. He soon got through the wood, but went on drilling. He drilled through glass, and suddenly, when he had pierced the bottom of a bottle, the brandy ran in a fine thin stream down through the hole in the table. He recognised his father's shoes under the table, and dared not think what would happen if he suddenly became visible again. But then with a thrill of joy he heard his father say, 'Empty,' and somebody else joining in, 'Hell, so it is.' Then everybody in the room got up.

Åke followed his father downstairs and when they reached the street he led him, though his father never noticed it, to a taxi-rank, and whispered the right address to the driver. During the whole journey he stood on the step to be sure they were really going in the right direction. When they were only a few blocks from home, Åke wished himself back—and there he lay again in the kitchen bench bed, listening to the car drawing up in the street. Not until it drove off again did he hear that it was not the right car: it had stopped next door. The right one must be still on the way; perhaps it had got into a traffic-jam, perhaps it had stopped in front of a cyclist who had fallen off; lots of things can happen to cars.

But at last one came which sounded like the right one. A few doors beyond Åke's house it began slowing down; it drove slowly past the next-door house and stopped with a slight squeak exactly opposite the right gateway. A door opened, a door banged, and somebody whistled as he rattled his money. His father never whistled, but one never knew; why shouldn't he suddenly take to whistling? The car started up and turned the corner, and afterwards the street was absolutely quiet. Åke strained his ears and listened down the stairs, but the front door never closed behind anybody coming in. The little click of the staircase light-switch never came. There was no muffled noise of footsteps on the way upstairs.

Why did I leave him so soon? Åke wondered. I might just as well have stayed with him all the way to the door, when we were so near. Now of course he's standing down there because he's lost his key and can't get in. Now perhaps he'll get angry and go away, and won't come back until the door's opened tomorrow morning. And he can't whistle, or he'd whistle to me or mum to throw down the key.

As noiselessly as he could Åke clambered over the edge of

the creaking bed and bumped against the kitchen table in the darkness; he stiffened all over his body as he stood there on the cold linoleum; but his mother's sobbing was as loud and as regular as the breathing of a sleeper, so she had heard nothing. He went forward to the window, and when he reached it he pushed the roller-blind gently aside and looked out. There was not a soul in the street, but the lamp above the gateway opposite was lit. It was lit at the same time as the staircase light, so it was like the lamp above Åke's own door.

Presently Åke grew cold and he padded back to the bench bed. To avoid bumping against the table he slid his hand along the draining-board, until suddenly his finger-tips touched something cold and sharp. For a while he let his fingers explore and then gripped the handle of the carving-knife. When he crept back into bed he had the knife with him. He laid it beside him under the blanket and made himself invisible again. After that he was back in that same room, standing in the doorway and watching the men and women who held his father prisoner. He realised that if his father was to be free he must release him in the same way as Viking released the missionary, when the missionary was bound to a stake to be roasted by cannibals.

Åke crept forward, raised his invisible knife and drove it into the back of the fat man next to his father. The fat man died and Åke went on round the table. One by one they slid down off their chairs without really knowing what had happened. When his father was free Åke took him down the many stairs and as he could hear no taxi about they walked very slowly down the steps, crossed the street and boarded a tram. Åke arranged it so that his father had a seat inside, hoping that the conductor wouldn't notice that his father had been drinking and hoping that his father wouldn't say any-

35

thing out of place to the conductor, or suddenly laugh out loud, just like that, without having anything to laugh at.

The song of the night tram rounding a bend forced its way inexorably into the kitchen, and Åke who had already left the tram and was lying in bed again noticed that his mother had stopped sobbing during the short time he had been away. The roller-blind in the next room flew up towards the ceiling with a fearful clatter, and when the clatter had died away his mother opened the window and Åke wished he could jump out of bed and run into their room and call out that she could quite well shut the window again, draw down the blind and go quietly to bed, for now he really was coming. 'On that tram, because I helped him get on to it.' But Åke knew it was no good doing that, as she would never believe him. She didn't know how much Åke did for her when they were alone at night and she thought he was asleep. She didn't know what journeys he made and what adventures he braved for her sake.

When later the tram stopped at the halt round the corner he stood by the window and looked out through the crack between the blind and the window-frame. The first people to come round the corner were two youths who must have jumped off while the tram was still moving; they were pretending to box with each other. They lived in the new house diagonally across the street. Passengers who had alighted were making a noise round the corner, and when the tram peered out with its lamp and rattled slowly across Åke's street, little groups of people came in sight and then vanished in different directions. One man with an unsteady gait, carrying his hat in his hand like a beggar, made straight for Åke's gateway, but it wasn't Åke's father; it was the porter.

But still Åke waited. He knew there were several things

round the corner that might delay a tram passenger: there were shop-windows, for instance—there was a shoe-shop there. Here his father might be standing to choose a pair of shoes for himself before he came in; and the fruit-shop had a window too, with hand-painted placards in it which lots of people stopped to look at because of the funny little men painted on them. But the fruit-shop also had a slot-machine that didn't work properly, and it might well be that his father had put in a twenty-öre piece for a packet of Läkerol for Åke, and now couldn't get the drawer open.

While Åke was standing by the window waiting for his father to tear himself away from the slot-machine, his mother suddenly left the bedroom next door and went past the kitchen. As she was barefoot Åke hadn't heard her, but she couldn't have noticed him because she walked on into the hall. Åke dropped the blind and stood motionless in total darkness while his mother searched for something among the coats. It must have been a handkerchief, for after a little while she blew her nose and returned to her room. Although her feet were bare, Åke noticed that she was walking especially quietly so as not to wake him. She shut her window at once and drew down the blind with a hard, quick pull. Then she lay down hastily on the bed and the sobbing began again, exactly as if she could only sob lying down, or had to start sobbing as soon as she did lie down.

When Åke had looked out at the street once again and found it empty except for a woman being embraced by a seaman in the gateway opposite, he crept back to bed, thinking —as the linoleum suddenly creaked underfoot—that it sounded as if he had dropped something. Now he was terribly tired; sleep rolled over him like mists as he walked, and through these mists he caught the clash of steps on the stairs—but going the wrong way: coming downstairs instead of up. As soon as he slipped under the covers he glided reluctantly but swiftly into the waters of sleep and the last waves that beat over his head were as soft as sobs.

Yet sleep was so brittle that it could not keep him away from all that preoccupied him when awake. Certainly he had not heard the taxi drawing up in front of the gate, the switching on of the staircase light or the steps coming upstairs, but the key that poked into the keyhole poked a hole in his sleep; instantly he was awake and joy struck down in him like a flash of lightning, sending a wave of heat through him from toes to forehead. Then the joy vanished as quickly as it had come, in a smoke of questions. Åke had a little game which he played whenever he awoke in this way. He played that his father hurried straight through the hall and stood between the kitchen and the bedroom so that both of them might hear him as he shouted,

'One of the chaps fell off a scaffolding and I had to take him to hospital; I've been sitting by him all night; I couldn't ring you because there wasn't a phone anywhere near.' Or, 'What do you know? We've won first prize in the lottery and I've come back late like this so's to keep you guessing as long as I could.' Or, 'What do you know? The boss gave me a motor-boat today and I've been out trying her, and early tomorrow morning we'll push off in her all three of us. What do you say to that, eh?'

But reality always happened much more slowly and never so surprisingly. His father couldn't find the hall light-switch. At last he gave up and knocked down a coat-hanger. He swore and tried to pick it up, but instead overturned a suitcase standing by the wall. Then he gave that up too, and tried to find a peg for his coat, but when he had found it the coat fell

38

on the floor just the same, with a soft thud. Leaning against the wall his father walked the few steps to the lavatory, opened the door and left it open, and switched on the light; and as so many times before Åke lay quite rigid listening to the splashing on the floor. Then the man switched out the light, bumped into the door, swore and entered the room through the drawn curtain, which rattled as if it wanted to bite.

Then everything was quiet. His father stood in there without saying a word; there was a faint creaking from his shoes and his breathing was heavy and irregular, but these two things only made it all even more hideously quiet, and in this quietness another flash of lightning struck down in Åke. It was hatred, this heat that surged through him; he squeezed the handle of the knife until his palm hurt, but he felt no pain. The silence lasted only a moment. His father began to undress. Jacket and waistcoat. He threw them on a chair. He leaned back against a cupboard and let the shoes drop off his feet. His tie flapped. Then he took a few steps further into the room, that's to say towards the bed, and stood still while he wound up the clock. Then everything was quiet again, as horribly quiet as before. Only the clock crunched the silence, like a rat—the gnawing clock of the drunk.

Then the thing the silence was waiting for would happen. His mother threw herself desperately round in bed, and the scream welled out of her mouth like blood.

'You devil, you devil—devil-devil-devil!' she shrieked, until her voice died and all was silent. Only the clock nibbled and nibbled and the hand clutching the knife was quite wet with sweat. The fear in the kitchen was so great that it couldn't be endured without a weapon, but at last Åke grew so weary from his deadly fear that unresistingly he plunged headfirst into sleep. Far down in the night he woke for a moment and through the open door heard the bed in the other room creaking and a soft murmur filling the room, and didn't quite know what it meant except that these were two safe noises which meant that fear had yielded for that night. He was still holding the knife; he let it go and pushed it from him, filled with a burning lust for himself, and in the very moment of falling asleep he played the last game of the night—the one that brought him final peace.

Final—and yet there was no end. Just before six in the evening his mother came into the kitchen, where he was sitting at the table doing his homework. She just took the arithmetic book from him and pulled him up from the bench with one hand.

'Go to your dad,' she said, dragging him out into the hall and standing behind him to cut off his retreat. 'Go to your dad and tell him I said he was to give you the money.'

The days were worse than the nights. The games of the night were much better than those of the day. At night one could be invisible and speed over the roofs to wherever one was wanted. In the daytime one was not invisible. In the daytime things took longer; it wasn't such fun to play in the daytime. Åke came out of the gateway and was not the slightest bit invisible. The porter's son pulled at his coat, wanting him to play marbles, but Åke knew his mother was standing up there at the window watching him until he should disappear round the corner, so he broke free without a word and ran away as if somebody were after him. But as soon as he turned the corner he began to walk as slowly as he could, counting the paving-stones and the splashes of spittle on them. The porter's boy caught him up but Åke didn't answer him, for one couldn't tell people that one was out looking for one's father because he hadn't brought the wages home yet. At last the porter's boy tired of it, and Åke drew nearer and nearer to the place he didn't want to get nearer to. He pretended that he was getting further and further away from it, but it wasn't true at all.

The first time, though, he went right past the café, brushing so close by the doorman that the doorman muttered something after him. He turned up a little side street and stopped in front of the building where his father's workshop was. After a while he passed through the entrance into the yard, pretending that his father was still there and that he'd hidden himself somewhere behind the drums and sacks for Åke to come and look for him. Åke raised the lids of all the paint-barrels, and each time he was just as much surprised not to find his father crouching inside. After hunting through the yard for half an hour at least, he realized at last that his father couldn't have hidden himself there, and he turned back.

Next to the café were a china shop and a watchmaker's. At first Åke stood looking in at the window of the china shop. He tried to count the dogs, first the pottery ones in the window, and then the ones he could see if he shaded his eyes and peered at the shelves and counters inside. The watchmaker came out just then and drew down the iron shutter in front of his window, but through the chinks in the shutter Åke could see the wrist-watches ticking away inside. He looked also at the clock with the Correct Time and decided that when the second hand had gone round ten times he would go in.

While the doorman was shouting at a fellow who was showing him something in a newspaper, Åke stole into the café and ran straight to the right table before too many people noticed him. At first his father didn't see him, but one of the other painters nodded at Åke and said,

41

'Your nipper's here.'

His father took Åke on his knee and rubbed his bristly chin against the boy's cheek. Åke tried not to look at his eyes, but now and again he was fascinated by the red lines in the whites of them.

'What d'you want, son?' his father asked, but his tongue was soft and slurry in his mouth and he had to say the same thing two or three times before he was satisfied.

'Money.'

Then his father put him gently down on the floor, leaned back and laughed so loudly that the others had to hush him. Still laughing he took the purse from his pocket, clumsily drew off the rubber band round it and hunted about for a long time until he found the shiniest one-crown piece.

'Here you are then, Åke, 'he said. 'Off you go and get some sweets for yourself.'

The other painters were not to be outdone, and Åke was given a crown by each of them. He held the money in his hand as, overwhelmed with shame and confusion, he picked his way out between the tables. He was so afraid that someone might see him running out past the doorman and tell tales at school, and say, 'I saw Åke coming out of a pot-house last evening.' But he paused for a moment in front of the watchmaker's window, and while the second hand swept ten times round its centre he stood pressed against the grille, knowing that he would have to play his games again tonight; but which of the two people he played for he hated more he couldn't tell.

Later, when slowly he turned the corner he met his mother's gaze from thirty feet up, and walked as lingeringly as he dared towards the gateway. Next to this was a woodmerchant's, and he was bold enough to kneel for a little and stare through the window at an old man putting coal into a black sack. Just as the old man finished Åke's mother came and stood behind him. She jerked him to his feet and took his chin in her hand, to find his eyes.

'What did he say?' she whispered. 'Did you funk it again?'

'He said he was coming back right away,' Åke whispered back.

'What about the money?'

'Shut your eyes, mum,' said Åke; and now he played the last of the day's games.

While his mother shut her eyes, Åke slipped into her out-stretched hand the four crown-pieces, and then dashed down the street on feet that slipped on the stones because they were so frightened. A rising shout pursued him along the houses, but did not stop him. On the contrary, it made him run all the faster.

SLEET

Sleet

No, there could never be another afternoon like that one.
There just couldn't, because only once is one nine years old,
topping carrots with a new Mora knife, having sleet in October,
with an aunt—or rather one's mother's aunt—arriving from
America at half past seven. We were sitting in the shed off
the stable, topping big muddy carrots. If one liked one could
easily imagine things: that it wasn't carrots that were losing
their tops, for instance, but schoolfellows one didn't like, or
wild beasts. Most often we didn't say anything, we just cut;
the green fronds fell between our feet and the beheaded
carrots flew in long curves into the chip basket.

There was a good smell of freshly-dug carrots. The tops
were wet, and when we got too dirty we washed ourselves with
them. As Alvar did to Sigrid if she didn't look out, climbing on
the upturned bucket, taking her by the neck and brushing her
face with the wet tops until she screamed and laughed. But
grandfather got angry and said to mother, who was sitting beside me on the stool that Alvar used when he shod the horses.

'Keep an eye on that youngster so he don't start any nonsense with the girl.'

Sigrid turned bright red and mother didn't answer. People
seldom answered when grandfather spoke; perhaps because
he was so old. I was almost the only one who did. When he
shouted at me my mother took my part. Alvar sat down on the
bucket again.

'You sit still in your chaff-cutter and mind your own
business, and I'll mind mine,' said Alvar to grandfather.

We hardly dared look, for sometimes grandfather would
get so angry that he went quite red in the face, and knocked

47

over his own chair and others too, and snatched his blue smock from the hanger in the kitchen and threw it on the floor and stamped on it. Now we just gave a quick look, but there was nothing special to see. Except that grandfather was sitting in the chaff-cutter, of course. 'Why can't you sit on a bucket like the rest of us?' said Alvar when we were going to start topping; but grandfather said if he couldn't sit in the chaff-cutter we could get on with it without him. So mother and Alvar helped to get grandfather up into the chaff-cutter. Sigrid laughed so much she had to run into the stable and shut the door behind her. Mother was annoyed, because she didn't like Sigrid laughing at grandfather, and she snapped at him for always making a laughing-stock of himself in front of people. But grandfather said if he couldn't sit in the chaff-cutter he wouldn't do the carrots either, and that was flat.

So there he sat; Alvar had filled the chute with carrots and put a pail underneath to catch the finished ones. But grandfather hardly ever made a good shot at the pail; almost always the carrots fell wide. It was the same at meals, when one heard mother say, 'At least stop dropping it all over yourself. Maybe we ought to buy you a bib.' At those times it was hard not to laugh, and if one laughed one had to leave the table. So it wasn't easy. It was worst when we had curds, because curds stuck in his beard and were almost impossible to get out, mother said. They set like cement.

But sometimes at meals grandfather would sneer, and tell mother she ought to be thankful she had a father at all. It's not every child that has one, he said, grinning at me. Then mother would jump up, knocking over her chair, run into her bedroom and bolt the door; and at such times it was impossible to do anything with her.

It was nice in the stable shed. The piles of carrot-tops

48

grew and grew. Rain fingered the shingle roof and Sigrid said it sounded so homelike. Yes, said mother, if one had a home it would be wonderfully homelike. The cat was jumping about in the hay, up in the loft. Suddenly he shot down, crept into the chaff under the chaff-cutter, and curled up. I killed a kitten once. I don't think it hurt at all, because it was so quick. In the stable the horses were gnawing their mangers.

'Alvar,' said grandfather. 'Go and see to the horses. They're good and hungry now.'

'Oh, them,' said Alvar. 'They've not been out of the stable all the week. Besides they're yours, so you can feed 'em yourself if you want to.'

Sigrid looked at grandfather open-mouthed to see whether he was going to get red in the face and start yelling again and mother looked too. But this time there was no trouble. Grandfather just sat in the chaff-cutter, topping his carrots. But Alvar hadn't topped any for a long time, so I stopped too and had a look at what he was doing. And Sigrid wasn't working either; she was watching Alvar. But mother went on; her knife flashed to and fro in the heap of carrots in her lap. She must have been very cross, for that was when she worked best, never saying a word. Mother was almost always cross, and with all of us at once. If it hadn't been for us, she used to say, she would never have been wearing herself out in the country, but would have found a good situation in some shop in town. In the daytime mother was nearly always cross with me, but at night when she thought I was asleep she used to lie and twist my hair round her fingers until I was afraid I should have curls.

Alvar had a carrot in his hand—a big one—and he had topped it and scraped it clean of earth. Now he was writing something on it with the point of his knife; he showed it to

49

Sigrid, who smirked. I wanted to go and look, but mother pulled me by the trousers and said I wasn't to go and meddle with what they were doing. But Alvar told me; Alvar was good to me, while Sigrid only pinched and nagged. He even let me look at the carrot. He had carved his and Sigrid's names on it, and the date. ALVAR BERG SIGRID JANSSON 18 10 1937. I asked him to put my name there too, and he took the carrot and added it. ARNE BERG, it said. Then he tossed it into the basket. But it seemed to me that Sigrid disliked having my name with theirs, for she gave me a dirty look. Alvar tickled her under the chin with some carrot-tops.

'Just think,' he said. 'Autumn will pass and then in the winter we'll go down into the cellar to fetch carrots for the animals, and we'll find this one, and we'll go out into the snow and eat it up.'

So I was probably not meant to be with them in this at all. But I was in so many other places: the cowshed, the lofts, the stable, and here in this shed. We were all here, for that matter. Grandfather and grandmother too were on the wall in the shed, but their names were so old you could hardly read them. Gustav and Augusta Berg, 10 8 1897. In 1914 mother came for the first time, and in 1918 Alvar. Then me in 1933 and Sigrid in 1936. Palestine was carved here too, on a beam. That had been last year, just before grandmother died. A tramp had slept the night in the shed, but moved on before anybody woke. While we were having our morning coffee grandmother went off to hunt for eggs, as she did every day. Suddenly she came rushing in, breathless, crying, 'Who do you think slept beneath our stable roof last night? Jesus— the Lord Jesus Christ.' But that evening another tramp came and I went with him into the shed to show him where the horse-blankets were, so that he could sleep warm. He wanted

50

to shake hands when he thanked me, but I was so afraid he might be lousy that I held back. Then he saw Palestine on the wall and said, 'Hell, if that old sod Palestine's been sleeping here, those bloody blankets will be crawling.' So Jesus was just a tramp after all, and lousy at that. And when grandmother was told the truth of it that evening she cried, and said I was too little to understand. But mother stood up for me and said I wasn't at all, because if a lousy tramp came along calling himself Palestine or Jerusalem or the Holy Land, that didn't mean he was Christ or the Apostle Paul, did it?

My carrots were nearly finished, so I took it easy. Mother's were soon done too, as well as Alvar's and Sigrid's. Only grandfather had a whole heap left. Mother went to the chaff-cutter to fetch some, but grandfather turned quite nasty and told her to leave his carrots alone. He was going to do them himself, so there.

'Want to be still at it when your sister comes?' asked mother; she snatched a bunch, and grandfather hit out at her with his knife. She was wearing one of Alvar's smocks, and the knife ripped up the sleeve. She stood looking at grandfather as if he weren't quite right in the head.

'Mind out now, dad,' she said, 'or you'll go doing something really daft—something you'll repent of all your days.'

For a while grandfather was subdued. There was silence. Only the rain jumped on the roof and the knives chopped at the carrots. At last I could contain myself no longer.

'Alvar,' I said. 'Tell me what the Atlantic's like.'

'The Atlantic,' said Alvar, pondering. 'In the Atlantic there are waves as big as houses.'

'What sort of houses?' I wondered. 'Red ones like ours, or yellow ones like the schoolmaster's?'

It seemed to me that if the waves were as big as houses

they must look like houses too. The whole Atlantic was one big parish with waves of two-storeyed houses and peasant cabins. And over them rode mother's aunt. Well, she wasn't riding any longer, because we'd had a letter from her the day she landed, and for four days after that grandfather was out on the steps ten times an hour, looking along the road to see if she was coming, but no Aunt Maja came. But one day another letter arrived, telling us to expect her in a week. Her brother-in-law would bring her in his car. Mother read the letter aloud after dinner, when grandfather had gone into his bedroom to lie down for a bit, and when she finished reading she was so angry that she tore it to pieces; of course, she exclaimed, being the poorest of the family we had to wait until the last—but not a hand's turn would she do to get the place straight for the old hag when she did come.

So nothing was done to smarten the place up for Aunt Maja; and yet we'd talked of nothing else since we got the first letter in the spring, saying she'd be with us in the autumn. We'll have a real do, I'd thought, and make the whole village sit up and stare. And now it was all to be a flop. Enough to make one feel cutting off one's thumb and throwing it among the carrots, so that Alvar and Sigrid would find it when spring came, and say 'Do you remember when Arne cut off his thumb? It was the day Aunt Maja came from America.'

'In another three hours your sister will be here,' mother told grandfather crossly, 'and there you sit in the chaff-cutter as if nothing was happening. I should have thought when you've not seen each other for twenty years you could at least have a shave.'

'I'll sit in the chaff-cutter or nothing. If me sister's too grand to come and see her brother except in a car and don't like her brother sitting in the chaff-cutter, then damn me sne can lump it and that's all about it.'

Sigrid laughed so much she had to run into the stable again. Grandfather was so excited he dropped his knife, and then mother took all his carrots and topped them in a single rush. I slid my knife into its sheath and went out into the yard, and looked down the road to see if the car was coming, but it was still much too early. Next I went over to the gate and carved my name and the date on one of the cross-bars. I shall never forget the day when it rained, and we topped carrots, and there was sleet, and the aunt from America came.

I sat on the kitchen settle and looked at the Atlantic in the atlas, although there wasn't much to be seen there. Not a single wave. So there was no knowing whether Alvar was making it all up. But now there was a great row in the yard, and looking out of the window I saw Alvar and mother coming along dragging grandfather between them. He was struggling, but it was no good. They got him in through the gate and up on the steps, and in the doorway he braced himself and kicked the door. But into the kitchen he had to come, and there they let him go.

'Now we're going to wash you,' said mother. 'Now at once.'

Alvar stood by the door so the old man couldn't slide out. Mother drew water from the cistern into the washing-up bowl. Alvar pulled off grandfather's smock. Besides that he was wearing only an undervest, and that came off too, so sweaty was he from struggling. Underneath, grandfather was quite yellow and thin. He fought, but they got him to the sink all the same.

'Arne, come here,' called mother—she sounded cross, so it was best to obey—'come along and soap his back.'

And that had to be done too, though it wasn't pleasant, because of the smell. I soaped his back until it couldn't be seen for lather. Then mother wiped it off with a rag. Alvar just helped to hold him. Sigrid sat on the sofa, grinning.

53

Then mother took the soap and rubbed it into his face and neck and ears, and he snorted and snuffled, but still couldn't get away. At last Alvar dipped his head into the bowl and grandfather got water down the wrong way and nearly choked.

'There now, dad, now you've only got to shave,' said Alvar at last, rubbing him dry with a towel.

Mother brought a clean shirt and pulled it over his head. Alvar led him to the table and sat him down on a chair. He took the shaving-glass from the chest of drawers, fetched the razor from the drawer and stropped it, brought a mug of hot water from the cistern and put it on the table, and knotted a towel round grandfather's neck to protect the clean shirt.

'And kindly don't spit on the floor while she's here,' said mother, chasing a moth through the kitchen.

Alvar lathered his grandfather's chin, picked up the razor and began to scrape.

'Hold still,' he snapped, 'or you can do it yourself.'

Grandfather sat looking at himself in the glass, and in the end he must have thought he looked a proper misery, for he began whimpering. 'Twenty years since I seen her,' he said, making such a face that Alvar nicked his chin.

'Hold still, can't you!' he barked.

'Twenty years,' grandfather went on. 'Fifty-three I was then, and she was thirty-three. The wife and I went to the station to see her off. Gave her lilacs and half-a-score of eggs. We howled so, the lot of us, the train pretty near went without her.'

I couldn't look on any longer, so I slipped out and walked along the river for a bit, throwing stones at the frogs and startling a poacher who had his boat among our reeds. It was dark, so I didn't see his face, and anyhow he turned it away as he rowed. After a bit I felt like carving something, so I took out my knife, ran up to the farmyard and into the stable shed. When I tugged open the door, Sigrid was lying on her back among the carrot-tops, with Alvar astride of her, biting her hand. Alvar jumped up and cursed me, so I slammed the door again and ran.

I didn't run indoors. What I felt was so extraordinary that I had to be alone with it. So I ran into the passage-way round the cowshed where we used to shoot the pigs, and sat on a milking-stool with my head in my hands. I tried to make the picture of Alvar and Sigrid let go of me, but I felt that to do this I should have to do something so dangerous and exciting as to make everything else seem small. I crept into the henhouse, scared away a hen that was sitting on her eggs and searched under the straw. The neighbour's boy had given me a cigarette, which I'd hidden here with a box of matches. But when I tried to light it I was so jumpy that I dropped the burning match, and the chaff of the henhouse floor caught fire a little. I poured a bowl of milk over it and put it out, but the smell of smoke still lingered.

I went and sat down again on the milking-stool in the passage-way. It was quite dark there; a little light pierced the chinks in the wall of the barn, making the threshing-machine with its wheels and belts look like a huge, spectral animal lurking in a dark den. Rain tapped on the eaves. Inside the byre the cows were munching, and that too sounded almost like rain. Then Sigrid came, with lantern and milk-pails. When she saw me she set down the pails and lantern on the passage floor and came towards me. Her face, lit from below, had such fearful shadows over it that I was terrified, and screamed. She grabbed my arm and pinched it, hard and long.

'If you tell Tora or the old man I'll squeeze your throat till you can't even squeak,' she said. Then she let me go, took up the lantern and the pails and went into the byre, where the cows rose rumblingly, mooing a little and rattling their chains like a row of shackled prisoners.

55

When I went indoors, grandfather was sitting on the settle looking utterly unlike himself. Mother had finally got him into his best clothes; the last time he'd worn them had been at grandmother's funeral the year before, and in the black suit of mourning he looked as pale as if all the blood had been drained out of him. A red cut on his cheek showed like a thin mouth, but apart from that he was quite white. He was tired, too, and no longer seemed aware of what was going on. I wondered whether he even remembered that in half an hour or so his only sister was coming; the sister he hadn't seen for twenty years.

Mother was combing her hair in front of the shaving-glass on the chest of drawers. She was wearing her best dress, and had found and put on a wrist-watch which didn't go, and which father must have given her. I switched on the radio; the weather forecast was going on: 'East Svealand and the coast of South Norrland. Rain during the day. Temperature below normal for the time of the year. Sleet in northern parts of the area.'

'What do they say?' asked grandfather feebly. 'What's the weather going to be?'

'Sleet,' I answered.

Alvar came in. He fetched the bootjack, pulled off his boots with a groan and put on shoes. I looked at the thermo-meter outside the window; I'd given it to grandfather for his seventieth birthday. He had always wanted one for the win-dow, but when he got it his sight was too poor for him to read it. 'You bought me one with too small figures on it, boy,' he said. 'Piddling little figures.' It was three degrees above freez-ing. The wind was rising, whining in the lilac hedge, and the rain beat hard against the window-pane. A lantern swayed over the yard from the cowshed; it was Sigrid on her way in with the milk-pails. I had a big blue bruise on my arm. I pulled down the roller-blind so as not to think about her.

When the clock struck, all of us except Sigrid were sitting and waiting. She was working the separator. Sigh-sigh, it said. Usually Alvar helped her, but not today. He was sitting at the table, looking at me in an odd way. Perhaps he too wanted to pinch me.

'Did you hear the weather?' Alvar asked, laying his hands on the table like great sandwiches.

'Sleet,' I answered for the second time.

It sounded so queer, so crazy. It didn't sound normal. But it went very well with all the other abnormal things that had been happening: grandfather in the chaff-cutter; mother and Alvar leading him across the yard; Sigrid lying on the carrot-tops with Alvar sitting on her; Sigrid pinching me; the near-fire in the henhouse; grandfather, mute and pale, on the settle.

Mother was sitting beside Alvar. She laid her hands on the table beside his, looked at them and sighed. The separator sighed too, sigh-sigh-sigh. All at once she looked at me to see whether I needed washing. She wrinkled her brows, my beautiful mother; she leaned across the table.

'Who gave you that nasty pinch on the arm?' she asked.

The separator slackened speed. Alvar glared at me. I was desperately afraid. There was nothing I feared so much as a thrashing. I turned my eyes away, looked behind me and saw grandfather sitting on the settle, just as white, staring before him with dumb, motionless eyes.

'Grandfather,' I said in a low voice, looking mother in the face.

Mother bit her lip. Alvar coughed. The separator speeded up; now it was singing its sighs. I glanced at grandfather but saw no change in him: he couldn't have heard. Time passed and the clock struck again. The separator sighed on, and it was because of that that we didn't hear anything until there came a knock on the outer door.

57

'Wasn't that a knock?' asked mother, and added, 'Dad, she's here. Aren't you going out to meet her?'

We all looked at grandfather, but he never moved; he just went on staring into vacancy, and none of us could bring himself to go out and open the door either. I pulled the blind aside and peeped out; a car was just trundling away through the gate, and it swished down towards the village. Then we heard steps in the hall—steps advancing slowly towards the kitchen door. Another knock. . . .

'Dad,' said mother, almost moaning. 'Now you *must*——'

The door opened. The aunt from America was standing on the threshold: a strange lady with hard, painted lines in her face. Her eyes were tired and her mouth was sunken, as if she had no teeth left.

'Good evening,' she said in a queer dialect, as she blinked at the light.

She came in. The separator had stopped in sheer astonishment. And now we all looked at grandfather. We wanted to see him jump up and fall on the neck of this strange woman —whom none of us knew because we were too young—and call her sister. But grandfather just sat where he was. The aunt from America caught sight of him and jumped in a startled sort of way. She paused in front of him with empty, outstretched hands.

'Gustav, is it you?' she said in a low voice, and none of us could think why she should have to ask such a silly question.

But grandfather didn't answer; grandfather didn't move a muscle of his face; it was as if he hadn't noticed anything. Then the aunt from America sank down on her knees in front of him—yes, on the floor, in all her fine clothes. She put her arms round grandfather's neck and tried to draw his head down to hers. But she couldn't.

58

'Gustav,' she whispered, 'it's me—Maja. You remember Maja!'

Then said grandfather, without even looking at her,

'Take care of yourself. There'll be rain and sleet tomorrow.'

The aunt from America let go grandfather's neck, stood up, pulled a long necklace out over her coat and fingered it helplessly, while her face twitched all over with weeping. She looked like one of those dolls you work on a string.

At last she turned away from us. 'Excuse me for a minute,' she said, before the sobs stifled her, and rushed out.

I took the stable-lantern and ran after her, thinking I must give her a light so that she wouldn't tumble into the river. She was standing in the rain and snow, crying. When I came with the lantern she took me by the arm and drew me with her. She talked rather funnily, I thought, and I didn't get it all.

'Are you the boy without any daddy?' she asked, among other things, looking long into my face.

I shut my eyes for a moment, and clenched my teeth. I could see well enough how everybody at school knew I hadn't got a father, but that it should be known all over America was something so frightful that I couldn't see how I was ever to get over it. However. We walked and walked and at last we were standing in front of the stable shed. And since we were there, I opened the door and we stepped in. It was warm and homelike; it smelt of stables, hay and carrots. I hung the lantern on the key of the stable door; the aunt from America —and this was surely odd—climbed over the carrot-tops, right to the back, and clambered up on to the chaff-cutter, exactly where grandfather had sat.

'The old thing's still here, then,' she said, and stroked it.

I climbed up and sat beside her. Then she began crying again. She took my hand and as she fondled it she kept crying in American and talking unintelligible Swedish words to me. The carrot-tops lay green and glossy below us, and the red carrots gleamed in their baskets.

'We've been topping and topping,' I told her, mostly for something to say. 'All day. But now it's all finished.'

The aunt from America threw her arms round me, and it didn't hurt as it did with mother; it felt soft and warm.

'Poor little boy with no daddy,' she said, and when I thought that the whole of America—all that huge America on the other side of the Atlantic—knew that Arne Berg of Mjuksand, Sweden, had never seen his father, I couldn't help it. I suddenly didn't see any carrot-tops any longer. Tears dripped slowly down on to the chaff-cutter.

'It wasn't so bad when grandmother was alive,' I said. 'It was like having two mothers then. But she died last year. Every morning she used to go out and look for eggs, and it was in April that she didn't come back. We had our coffee and afterwards we went out and looked, and here she was kneeling by the chaff-cutter.'

'*Por liddel boy*,'* said the aunt from America—whatever she might mean by that—and hugged me close.

'But if you're going to sleep here, auntie,' I said, 'don't be afraid because it says Palestine on the wall. It wasn't Jesus who came here. Shall I carve your name there too?'

'Not yet,' she said, 'but soon.'

She passed her soft little hand over my face.

'You're crying,' she said.

'I'm not.' I rubbed and rubbed until the carrot-tops glinted green and freshly cut again in the lamplight. 'It's just sleet.'

*Swedish-American-English in original.

WHERE'S MY ICELAND JERSEY?

Where's my Iceland Jersey

Ho, ho; met like gentry, with Ulrik standing at the corner of the station-building in greased boots and his best hat—the one with the broadest brim—staring down-hearted-like over the station yard. Crape band he had, too, and a black rosette. Behind him the horse was nuzzling at the flowers in the border. We was to drive in the spring cart and I hadn't done that since I was a youngster. Met like gentry, just because dad was dead. Other times it's been walk, walk, walk, though the mud come over your boot-tops. 'Cept for mum's funeral, that is.

Him all over—couldn't walk over to meet a fellow, could he, though he seen which carriage I come out of. And all I had to carry, too, what with the wreath and the bag of *brännvin*. Maybe I could a put the wreath in the van—though you can't be sure: look what happened to mum's. They mucked it up so on the railway, Old Nick himself couldn't a put it straight, and I could a sunk through the ground for shame at the funeral, trying to spread the ribbons, like, to hide the flowers. And as for saying anything to them railway chaps—why, it's a waste of breath. They just blames you back and leaves you standing there like a stuck calf.

Well anyway, he showed he seen me, Ulrik did. Salutes and puts on a grin, yokel-style—but what can you expect? The iron-plater chap was there, too, Saturday-tight as usual; he stopped and wanted to talk. He seen the bag all right and guessed what was in it. 'Sorry to hear about your loss,' he says. 'Went off quick, didn't he? Saw him the day before and he was doing fine!' Well, it's no news to anybody that dad took a drop in his old age, but no need to shout it all over the station. I wondered if he'd been invited. They used to drink together, him and the old man, but no call to ask him to the funeral on that account.

My crape band had slipped crooked. Lost the other one, I had: out drunk one Saturday and when I come home it was gone. It's not that you grieve with your clothes, exactly, but to go and lose it on a blind! Made me feel small, though it was a month after the funeral. This one's too big too, or maybe I'm too thin for 'em. Anyhow it keeps slipping down over me wrist. Looks proper yokel, somehow.

And Ulrik. I went up to him, and what's he do? Never shook hands, though I put me bag down all ready. And not a word, though I says Hullo twice. But that's how he's always been, Ulrik. Sort of locked up and sulky.

'You see to the wreath then, Ulrik boy,' I told him. Well, I mean, we're brothers, aren't we? No good getting awkward till you has to. The cardboard box with the wreath in it just fitted in snug under the back seat. But the bag—well, I thought I'd hang on to that meself. Ulrik clicked his tongue and old Blenda lumbered round with her mouth full of the station-master's flowers. 'Put down the bag, boy,' says Ulrik. But I know what happened at mum's funeral. Young brother Tage had to show off and help carry. Clonk went the bag when he slung it against a gatepost, and two of the bottles cracked. Had to gallop out and scrape some more *brännvin* together, middle of Saturday afternoon. So this time I thought I'd hang on to the bag meself.

Warm here. Asked if they'd had any rain. Not for a month past, he said. Fine for October. 'We got the cards off a bit late,' said Ulrik, 'but you got yours all right, I suppose?'

The cards. We was driving past the bank now, and the doctor's house, and the café with the miniature golf course.

That's where Frida used to work. Not a bad set-up, that wasn't; used to go in the back way and the drinks was free. While it lasted. It was always a saving, having Frida. 'You got it in time, I expect,' says Ulrik—mostly to put his own mind at rest. But he never did have much to say for himself, Ulrik didn't, and never wrote a line without he had to.

So the letter arrived all unexpected on the Sunday. I'd been to the races all day and won a hundred and fifty, and that don't happen often. So a chap could be forgiven for not being stone cold sober. My old woman put the letter on the electric meter, and fussed about and watched how I took it the minute I got in the door. Like when mum died, only then we got a proper letter first, from Lena my little sister who's at the sanatorium now; and that was quieter like. So I opened it and kept reading and reading, and it was some time before I could take it in. And well, you do feel a bit small, getting news of a death when you're tiddly, and the wife couldn't let it go without passing the remark. But I give her her answer. The old man himself was never one to turn his back on a glass, I tells her, and how did she know he died sober? Only it did feel a bit queer—like at mum's funeral when I went out to borrow a drop for the dinner and came back in the evening as gay as a grig and felt queasy all through the burial service next day.

'You got the clothes all right,' my old woman said. 'All except the crape arm-band; we'll have to buy that, 'cause you went and lost the other one on that blind.' I'll never hear the last of that, not till my dying day.

A car passed us—a new Chev, brand new. I told my brother but he didn't know what a Chev was, nor a Chevrolet neither hardly, for that matter. Shame about Lena, he said, squeezing it out, like; shame she couldn't come home for it. And it was, too; there was always something a bit special about young sister Lena. Never sulky and cross-grained like Ulrik, and not like her big sister neither, so stuck-up and grand as she is since she took and married that radio dealer. Running about in national dress on Sundays and joining the Women's Army Corps. My own sister! Looks down at me, I know that; I'll never forget the rumpus she made at mum's funeral just 'cause I happened to slip up a bit that morning. 'I got a brute for a brother'—that's what she come out with. No, so far's I was concerned she could stay away. But Lena, she was something else again. More like me: not afraid of a chat, not a bit proud and never looked down on a fellow in her life. And she has to go and get TB working in that old sod Lundbom's place, just because he wouldn't have a fire in the room. I wouldn't wish me worst enemy the job of housekeeping for that swab.

The Chev came back. Must have been down to the 'Tourist' and turned. People come out here all the way from town just to soak at the 'Tourist'. I thought I might slip out that evening, though I hadn't forgot what happened at mum's funeral. All I got was a bawling-out afterwards. And trouble. The Chev pulled up, but not because Blenda was scared. Blenda's been in the army and hauled guns for bombardiers. The cart stopped and the car stopped, and who should wind down the window but baker Holmgren. A bit balder since mum's funeral, but the same merry old nose. Face was redder too, but that might a been sunburn. Might a been.

'Sorry to hear of your loss,' says baker Holmgren, though he didn't look it. 'Sad about your dad. But if you got nothing better to do tonight, come along over. Not often we sees you in these parts,' he says. 'No, not since mum's funeral,' says I, doing me best to look solemn; but that weren't easy when

66

I thought of all the larks we'd had together, the Baker and me. The amount of *brännvin* we'd drunk between us would have kept me tight for six months, at a pinch. 'Have to see about that; just have to see,' I told him, not wanting to promise anything in front of Ulrik. But Ulrik clicked his tongue and waved his whip, and the old mare took off in second, with the hell of a jerk. But I'd got the bag steady between me knees, so no harm done. The Chev started up and drove on.

'Nice car,' I said, and I couldn't help wondering where Baker found the dough for it. Last time he borrowed a ten-crown note off of me, to get his old woman's shoes out of hock. She hadn't been out of the house for three days, or so he said. But he says a lot, the Baker. Otherwise he's all right.

'He got a win on the pools first,' Ulrik said, 'and then in a lottery. So he'll soon drink himself under ground.' Envy, that sounded like. Sulky and envious, that's Ulrik. He swung the whip while Blenda jogged along down to the 'Tourist'. The brewers' vans stand outside there. 'Got any beer at home? If not we'll pick up a case here,' I said. But that made Ulrik wild. Cracked his whip so the old mare was out on the bridge in a couple of jumps. 'Can't you think of nothing else, even when dad's dead?' he said. 'Beer and *brännvin*, that's all you got in your head.' Could have found an answer to that, of course. Could have reminded him how I'd sent snuff-money home to the old man for eight long years—and then look at all the dresses mum got from my old woman! So there was other things in my head, all right, if I cared to take that line. And besides, I meant well with that case of beer. I remembered what happened at mum's funeral. There was nothing but water by the end, and who had the disgrace of it but Ulrik and meself? I could a reminded him of that if I'd cared to.

But I never was one to rake up old scores. Though I

67

always say mum's affairs was handled pretty fishy after she went. Not a lot of water in the river, so the stones was high and dry. Say what you like about Blenda, she can shift. But she was one of dad's buys. Ulrik was chewing something over. Had a job to bring it out, but he done it in the end. Spat it out like a fishbone: 'How are you getting along with your old woman these days, then? With Elinda?'

Innocent questions gets an innocent answer. I told him she'd had a cold, and how she caught her skirt in the spokes of the bike, so she tumbled off and ricked her arm. Else everything was fine—and that shut him up. I knowed very well what he meant. A man's not a fool. Never was. I could see they knowed all about it here at home: Lydia'd have seen to that, if no one else. Or that man of hers, that bag of lard, who drives round in a van palming off old radio sets on the customers. What sort of a business it is he's got so fat on— well, the less said the better. I *could* say a good deal.

But he'd turned quiet, Ulrik had. Not easy to know what he was thinking. He always was a sly one. Sly and sulky. There was parasols in the garden of Carlsson's café, and Grindstugan had a miniature golf course. Might have a game later on. If anybody kicked up about that, there was always an answer. Dad was never one to pull long faces. 'Come into my room, boy,' he says to me that evening, 'but don't let 'em see you.' And then he took two glasses out of the chiffonier and a drop of brandy he'd saved. 'You're all right, son,' says dad. 'You're not too big for your boots.' Always fair, dad was, and he knowed what a fellow was made of. And never turned his back on a glass, though he was seventy-two then. So now dad was gone, what was there to go home for any more?

Only maybe I ought to cheer Ulrik up a bit. It couldn't always have been a bed of roses for him either. All alone there now. Never had the sense to get himself a wife. And the housekeeper she left. Course, they said dad was at her something fierce after mum died—but people will talk. And what did they want with a housekeeper after that? Mum she was bedridden, so of course *she* needed looking after, but dad was on his legs to the last—he could always toss a bite of grub together, could dad, old as he was. Good job the boy stayed on, else Ulrik couldn't a managed, for all they go on about how strong he is.

Hardly a soul in the village. There was a tall chap with a paper bag standing by the side of the road, waiting till we'd gone by. A tramp, I suppose, 'cause when we'd passed him he nipped in through Petterson's gate—Petterson the shopkeeper. He took the wrong turning there, though, 'cause Petterson don't have a penny to spare for any tramp. Mean, he is, like all the rest round here. With dad it was different— he always had a bite and a bed for a tramp. Mostly because he wanted someone to talk to, of course. He was a cheerful soul, was dad. But as for Ulrik, you couldn't never get a word out of him. So when we was sitting together after mum's funeral, dad said, 'if you want a drink in this house you got to get it on the sly.' Not that Ulrik would ever say anything, but he'd glare at you fast enough. Glare so it scorched you. He'd have to be real wild before you'd get a word out of him.

That was the last time I ever spoke to my old dad, so I remember it ever so clear. They ought to know, all of 'em, that dad wasn't the sort to look sideways at a fellow. Every time I come home after going to live in town I has to hear all about what a fine fellow Ulrik is: does the work of three, they say, while I enjoys meself in town. And never swears only when he's angry. Don't smoke and hasn't tasted a drop since his military service. There was that time on dad's seventieth birthday. Dad and I put some *brännvin* into a bottle of pop, and poured it into Ulrik's glass. Ulrik was thirsty and tossed it straight down, not knowing. Struth, what a pantomime! Ulrik he dashed out and threw it all up on the grass, and come in again and roared at us like a ruddy mastiff. Still, a drop or two must have stayed in him.

Next we met the schoolmaster. He was new, and so high and mighty he couldn't hardly bring himself to tip his hat. Old Jacob who had the job in my day, he was dead, Ulrik told me. Sat on a chair in the garden and died. 'The old ones are going,' said Ulrik. 'First mum, and then Jonsson at the mill. Drowned in the mill-stream last autumn.' I remembered hearing it on the radio: 'Elov Jonsson of Kvarnlunda was drowned on Tuesday night. He was eighty-two.' And an old woman was run over on the main road that same week, but I didn't know her. 'Then Jacob,' Ulrik went on. 'And Stenlund got cancer and ended his days in the workhouse. And then dad.'

A cyclist come up behind us and rung his bell, and Ulrik slowed up and pulled over to the side. He shoved his hat up off his forehead and looked about—looked back and to the side, just as if we had to be alone to talk about dad. Quite chatty he was by now. That don't happen often, so when it does you remember it. When Wiklund's bull got loose and broke young Tage's rib with his horn, Ulrik went on all night about compensation and the law. It surprised us all. It was news to us that Ulrik could talk. And I remember when mum was to be buried: Ulrik went on and on so, we thought he'd never stop.

Dad was going to see the nurse that day, Ulrik told me. 'Dad was a bit hard of hearing, as you know, and as soon's he got up he said to me "Ulrik", he says, "I'm off to see nurse before I goes stone deaf. I ain't heard you say a word all the week, Ulrik," says dad. And he gets out the bike that morning and away he goes. I was driving to the smithy to fetch the plough, and while I was harnessing Blenda I see him coming, pushing his bike. "Hold on a bit, dad!" I shouts through the stable door. "I'll take you. I'm off to the blacksmith and it's not much further to nurse's." Because he hadn't ridden that bike the whole year. First he couldn't get his leg over, he was that rheumaticky. "Be blowed to that," says dad. "I'm spry enough to ride that little bit of a way." So I let him go, though I didn't like it. When I got to the forge the blacksmith was standing in the yard and yells at me when I come in the gate, "What do you want to let your dad go so far on his own for?" "Far?" I says. "No distance to nurse's." "Nurse's!" he says. "I been into town and come back with the brewer and I saw your dad a long way out on the road to Mon. Wobbling so, he could easy have an accident." So then I knowed what he was up to,' says Ulrik, 'Mon's where that iron-plater chap lives, and we all know he's not one to refuse a drink, nor ask where it come from, neither. And there was a bulge in dad's coat—I remembered that when I thought about it. I took the plough home, and when I got in I went into the bedroom to have a look in the chiffonier, but it was locked and the key gone. He'd turned suspicious in his old age, though I'm not one to go poking in other people's chiffoniers,' said Ulrik. 'I stopped in the shed all that day, mending pitchforks and mattocks, seeing as we'd be lifting potatoes in another week. Had the door open, so I could keep an eye on the road. But noon come and coffee-time, and no dad. And the boy he hung round the wood-pile all day looking sly, so he knowed what was going on right enough.

'At last I took the bike,' says Ulrik, 'and went up towards the village, but not a sign of him. I looked in at nurse's just to make sure, and when she opened the door she grabbed my hand so I was quite took aback. "Yes, your dad's here," she says, and I was glad he hadn't lied altogether. But when I went in he was lying on the bed with his head bandaged, snoring fit to bust. "I was looking out the window," says nurse, "and there he comes on his bicycle, wobbling about from side to side, and I thinks to meself he's for it. And then he give a lurch and tumbled off, and baker Holmgren was coming along in his car just behind, but he managed to stop," says nurse. "He helped me to carry him in, and it's a wonder he ever got on the bike at all, drunk like he was".'

That's what Ulrik said. Only I didn't see why he had to drag in all that about the drunkenness just now, so near the funeral. It would give Lydia and her chap a bit more to natter about. I remember how they carried on at mum's funeral, just because I'd been good enough to bring along my whole ration of spirits. But he hadn't finished yet, because he let Blenda crawl along like a snail. Gave us a spavined sort of a look, that did, going so slow.

'I asked her how he was,' Ulrik said, 'and nurse shook her head and said he'd have to rest a few days, and if I could get him home she'd come and have a look at him next morning. Her whole room was smelling of *brännvin*—a nice thing, middle of the potato crop and all. I took the bike and rode home. Dad's bike was at the bottom of nurse's steps; the handlebars was twisted, else it was all right. I waited till it was a bit darker—didn't want the whole village staring just because of dad,' said Ulrik, 'and then I put the flat cart to and drove up to nurse's. Dad was sleeping like a log when we carried him out, nurse and me. The boy he sniggers when we come home and laid dad on the couch in his bedroom. Didn't fancy undressing him, so I just spread a blanket over him and went and milked and saw to the horses. But when people come for their milk that evening they knew all about it right enough, and grinned, and said he was never one to turn his back on a glass—only all the same, at that age. . . . So I had quite a bit to put up with on dad's account. That night I thought I heard something funny in his room, so I got up and went in and struck a match over him. And I was scared,' said Ulrik. 'I switched on the electric, but he was dead. The boy drove off to fetch nurse, but she just stopped in there alone with dad a few minutes and then come out to us in the kitchen and said nobody would a thought it would be so quick.'

We were passing the nurse's place just then; she was standing in the window staring at us—the window she was at when dad came and tumbled off and fell asleep for the last time. Just there on the road, it was, outside Jacob's hedge. Many's the time I ran along there as a kid, stepping just on that very spot; used to slide there, winter time. And even then it was fated: there your dad's going to fall off his bike and bash his head in. Ulrik cracked his whip and Blenda started off like a rocket, but all the way to the bend by the boarding-house I sat twisted round, looking at that little stretch of road between the nurse's white house and Jacob's hedge. It was like looking at dad's grave. That's what made me realise he was dead.

And yet opposite the boarding-house was the churchyard, and the door of the mortuary chapel was open. You couldn't see that from the road when mum was buried: the maples hid it, because it was in July. And just where the wall began Ulrik slowed up and took off his hat, and sat with it on his knee until we'd passed the church. Old Ulrik and his notions. As if it could help dad to take off your hat when you passed the mortuary. Somebody closed the door then—shut dad in—

73

but it didn't feel the same as just now. It didn't feel like it did looking at the road. And it's funny, but when I thought of dad it didn't feel like that either. There was always so much life in dad, so when you think about him you just think of all the fun you had together. The morning of the day mum was buried I took and shaved dad with my safety, and dad was so pleased he nearly cried. 'If only Ulrik would do this,' he said, 'but Ulrik don't give a damn if me hands get so shaky I cut me throat when I try and shave.'

Ulrik was staring at my hat, but if he wanted to get it off he'd have to pull it off himself. In the boarding-house we'd just passed I once knew somebody called Irma. Not bad, either. We used to meet in the wood behind in the evenings, and she'd bring boarding-house food with her in a cloth. In those days a man wanted for nothing. But then Fru Lund came, and that was the end of that. And Irma took up with a lieutenant who'd lived in the boarding-house for four years. 'He's no cupboard-lover,' she says to me, right in me face. The things I put up with! Got some of me own back, though.

On with your hat now, Ulrik—on with it. And he put it on exactly as we was passing the last grave in the churchyard, and Blenda got such a cut she bolted down the hill. The blacksmith was hanging over his gate looking good and tight. Only a little way to go now. Across the stream where I thought you could fish when I was a nipper, past the manse and on to our land. 'Maybe I should a left the wreath there,' I said to Ulrik. But answer me? No. He was so sour his moustache drooped. There was a car standing in the farmyard; you could see it at once, and then that lout of Lydia's came out on to the steps. He had a white shirt on, and was puffing at a cigar. The place looked pretty small—gets smaller every time I come home. Even at mum's funeral there didn't seem much of it left, and now it had shrunk to nothing, you might say.

Ulrik was staring at me from the side. Expect he was thinking: 'Take a good look. It's the last chance you'll get of looking at my home free gratis and for nothing.' Lydia's fatty opens the gate for us to drive in, and of course I had to say hullo. I handed down the bag and got out, and I was going to do the proper thing and clap him on the shoulder. But the fellow started as if he'd been stung and walked off with the bag. Thought I was drunk, of course. And I suppose his shirt was too white for a plain, honest hand to touch. Ulrik drove on to the well and let Blenda drink from the tub. I wasn't going to run after the radio dealer: he could slow up for me. And he did, too. Mostly so's he could brag about his car.

'Yes, I've got a new one now,' he said, just as if anybody'd asked him. 'A six-seater this time. Pontiac. Ideal for business trips.'

So business was going well for the old swab. At the little gate he pulled himself together, though, and opened it, and put on an air and said he must offer his sympathy. Lydia came out on the steps. She'd got fat and heavy, but at least she wasn't wearing that Army Corps uniform, nor national dress neither. Hugged me, she did, till I thought my back would break; hung her head over my shoulder and hiccuped, while her chap stood by, staring as if he was at the circus. Well, we got inside at last, and to start with everything was as usual: dad's clothes hanging in the lobby and his cap on the shelf; dented, it was, and covered with dust. And when I come in the kitchen you didn't notice anything missing. Only the longer I stood there with Lydia hiccuping the emptier it got. The bedroom door never opened and no dad come rolling out with his braces dangling. And there was the calendar—nobody'd bothered with that since he went.

75

8 October, it said, so he hadn't forgotten to tear it off on that last day. Lydia hiccuped and Ulrik slammed the stable door and the radio chap stood holding the bag as if there was a bomb in it at least. And when it got too miserable I said how empty the house felt. You can feel there's something missing, I said.

That turned the taps on proper with Lydia. She really started then. She sat down on the kitchen settle and rummaged in her handbag for a handkerchief. The radio fellow said he'd take my bag down to the cellar for the present, and it was on the tip of me tongue to say I'd counted 'em, so he needn't try anything on. But I let it go, for Lydia was snivelling away, and by the end I found it hard to control myself. Specially when I sat down beside her and she butted her head against my shoulder. Still, she gave over crying after a bit, and began talking and carrying on. 'Just as we was beginning to do so well,' said Lydia. 'Just when we could a had dad to live with us, or help him with money and that, then he goes and leaves us.' Yes, she sounded really put out because dad had had the sauce to die before she had time to help him.

Well, it was hard luck on Lydia—damned hard luck, and so I told her: 'You always was unlucky, Lydia,' I said. 'When you got to the point when you could a put mum into hospital she up and died. And by the time you're doing so splendid that you can lend a chap a bit of money to send Yngve to the Tech., then I expect I'll up and die too,' I said.

Lydia stops hiccuping then and just glares, and her eyes was angry, you could see that. She got to her feet quick as lightning and went out of the kitchen, every ounce of fat on her wobbling with rage. Going out to tell tales, that's what it was—tell her radio·chap what a brute her brother was. So it seemed to me a good idea to keep out the way for a bit. I went into his old room and shut the door so nobody wouldn't disturb me. For it was here I had my last evening with dad, two summers ago. It was stuffy in here, and smelt of dust, but it was there on that couch I sat, with dad beside me. The window had been open then, but dad shut it in case anybody was listening. Oh, he was suspicious, sure enough: Ulrik was right there. And it felt funny to be sitting here remembering. Thinking that he'd never be here again. On the table that we'd sat by when mum was buried I saw the local paper with his death notice in it. A fine big one it was, so Ulrik hadn't stinted. He must have remembered the ticking-off he got over mum's notice, which was just nothing at all—a measly little bit of a space you needed a magnifying glass for. Ulrik said it weren't his fault and he couldn't know what it would look like in the paper. But it was meanness. Plain meanness.

'Oh, so there you are.' Ulrik had opened the door, looking suspicious. Suppose he thought I'd shut meself in to have a nip from my pocket flask, all on my own. Lydia was there too, but not so much as a glance from her, so I knew I'd given her what was good for her. But it wasn't me they came for. It was dad's clock, dad's cuckoo-clock what he carved himself when he was young. It hung over his bed and he was always proud of it. Whenever anybody new came to the place they always had to go into the bedroom first off and see dad's clock. He wound it himself. He kept the key locked up in the chiffonier so no one else could get at it, and it was because he thought a lot of me that he once let me wind it up, as a nipper. But he was drunk at the time, and he said beforehand, 'If you overwind it, you young limb——!'

So Lydia needn't come and boast that she's wound up the cuckoo-clock, nor yet Ulrik neither, for that matter. Well, and to be sure they didn't. But Ulrik told Lydia, and me too if I'd listen, that it stopped the night he died—at the very minute, said Ulrik. And all three of us looked at the dial. Half-past one it was, or twenty-three minutes past, to be precise.

The weight Lydia'd put on! What a sight. She'd got so stout since mum's funeral she could hardly get through the bedroom door. But she did. She come in and stood by dad's bed and said if Ulrik couldn't get the clock to go, Nils could. That's her husband. Nils was ever so handy. She's got so grand now she can't call him Nisse any more. Next time we meet, if there is a next time, she'll be saying Mr Johansson. We did look at each other then, Ulrik and I, for at least we was agreed on one thing: if the clock stopped when dad died we wouldn't set it going again—not until after the funeral, anyway.

They was rustling up the grub now in the kitchen. The neighbour had lent his eldest girl to Ulrik for these few days, and a fine girl she looked. Like Frida at her best. I took her arm quite lightly, as she stood at the stove turning the pancakes, but then I saw Lydia glaring—well, I mean, it was plain silly. She didn't eat with us; she sat on the settle and read the paper. A nip of *brännvin* would have gone down well, but the radio chap didn't seem inclined for it, so I thought I'd better not try. Not a word spoken at first. Seemed like nobody quite liked to, so then I said it was a hell of a nice car Nils had got himself.

And Nils brightened up until I began to feel hopeful about that drink after all. And then that Lydia goes and ruins it. She fancied I was getting at him, and snaps out that some people don't spend all the money they earn on spirits, so of course they can afford to have things nice. So that was one in the eye, though I hadn't said one word about *brännvin* since I set foot in the house. I'd been disgraced before, many's the time, but in front of a stranger—well, it wasn't right. The girl never looked up from her paper, but she'd heard all right. You could see she'd heard. So I got to thinking that a whole evening here would be just plain hell. I could have answered back—reminded her that some people had sent snuff-money home to dad for eight long years, and frocks for mum in her day. So if anybody wanted to draw up a balance they was welcome. But you can't stir things up, or there's no end to it.

So after dinner I went down to the cellar where Ulrik had put the cardboard box with the wreath in it. There was a few more there on the floor: Ulrik's and Lydia's, and Lena had sent flowers too. And a man don't want to be petty, but it was a measly little wreath Lydia and Nisse had bought. Not even a decent ribbon to it. As for Ulrik's, a proper yokel's wreath it was, but you can't get the same here as what you can in the market-town. Lena just sent flowers, but pretty ones, and you couldn't blame her for not affording a wreath when she's been laid up in the sanatorium for close on eighteen months. There was nothing from young Tage, but he'd be bringing it with him on the night train. I didn't suppose anybody but me would a thought of mum, but I brought her a few flowers in the cardboard box, and I picked them up to take to the churchyard that evening. I opened the bag, too, and slipped a half-pint bottle into my pocket. Not that I was going to baker Holmgren's, but a fellow might meet an old crony and it would be nice to have something to offer him.

They was all sitting in the kitchen as if they was in church when I come up again, with the poor girl washing up and nobody helping her. So I grabbed a cloth to go and dry. But 'None of that nonsense now,' says Lydia. 'We know all about you and your goings-on, and no decent girl would accept help from you.' And of course the girl wanted to be

79

decent, so she turned red in the face and snatched away the cloth and whooped 'No thank you'. And there I stood like a blackguard. So God knows what they'd been saying about me while I was down in the cellar.

Well anyhow, I took mum's bunch and said I was going to mum's grave. But Lydia got anxious, I could see, for she says quicklike that Nils could quite well drive us to the churchyard, Knut dear. And she was wonderful interested in mum's grave all of a sudden, but it's only that she don't want to let a fellow out on his own. She was scared it would be like last time. Not for my sake—she don't give a damn about me—it was the scandal she was thinking of. For there had been a bit of talk last time about my going and getting tight the night before mum's funeral. But Nils could chase himself, and Lydia too, and Nils was in the bog-house at the time, so before he got back I nipped out the door and took the short cut through the paddock so's not to meet him.

A fine family! Hardly trust a man to go to his mother's grave even. And that nasty tone from Ulrik: 'You can borrow a can and a rake at the churchyard, if you ever get there.' If I ever get there! What did they think I was going to do with the flowers—chuck 'em in the river? Eight crowns they cost me, so nobody couldn't say a man hadn't done the right thing by his parents. If everybody did as much, I could a stood the nagging better.

It was grand for October, no denying. In a field up near the wood they was burning potato-haulm. The Wiklunds had got themselves a lifter; it was standing at the corner of the byre. If Ulrik had more go in him he'd go shares with Wiklund in the lifter, and then he wouldn't have to split himself so, working. I tell him that every time I go home— but there, if Ulrik wants to slave himself to death it's none of my business. There were leaves on the road. It was getting dusk, so I hurried to reach the churchyard before it was quite dark. In the window of the manse I saw the pastor smoking his pipe—a clergyman smoking a pipe! It looked funny. Easy going along the road, but not for the blacksmith. He was reeling this way and that; any minute now he'd be in the ditch. Hard for him to keep sober, but he's a decent chap and he was one of the last to see dad. I felt I ought to have a word with the iron-plater, though, before I went back to town. Drinking's all very well, but to send dad home when he weren't up to it, that's something I ought to talk to him about.

Not many people, but there was dancing at the Pavilion, even now in the middle of October. It said so on the poster. I'd have gone there, I expect, if dad hadn't been dead. Too dark for golf. No sense paying one-fifty and not find a single hole. So I kept to the proper side of the road and opened the churchyard gate. The family grave's easy to find, and that was lucky, for it was getting too dark to go hunting for it. It's just opposite the mortuary door, so at mum's funeral we carried the coffin past the open grave into the church, and then back the same way. Sweaty business it was, but then it was the middle of July. Heatwave.

There was one vase on the grave, with a few flowers rotting in it. So Ulrik wasn't putting himself out much. It hadn't been raked either. I couldn't see to do that just then, though; too dark. Still, it looked pretty good now: nobody couldn't say they wasn't nice flowers. But in the mortuary-chapel the fellows was still hammering. Damn funny notions you get: lay off that, I wanted to say, you'll wake dad. Damn silly. It was the coffin decorations they was working on, because the boy from the market-garden looked out for a minute. But he didn't recognise me. Just as well. Didn't feel like looking in there this late. When they get the headstone up on mum's grave—mum's and dad's grave it'll be called now—it'll look quite decent. Good position, too; the best, really.

It was dark now, and the wind hissing through the leaves. Squeaking from the church roof. What about going somewhere? Could sit for a bit, anyhow, in some place or other. Might see somebody I knew. Ought to show meself too, while I was home, else it'd be 'Oh, Knut—he's so big-headed now he won't be seen in the village, except driving from the station and back.'

Or baker Holmgren. How well I remembered what happened when mum was buried. Had to go round to the old Baker to borrow *brännvin* instead of the bottles young Tage busted, and stayed there half the night. God knows where we didn't get to before I come home. Always pretty lively at old Baker's. Still, it would be nice to hear a bit about dad. After all, it was the Baker who come up behind him in the car and nearly run him over. So if I went to see him it would be to ask about dad. And Lydia and Nisse and the whole lot of 'em could do what they liked about it. What did they care about dad when he was alive? But now, when he was lying the other side of that door over there, they went into their act, striking attitudes and carrying on. While he was alive nobody but me had a thought for him. Sent money every month for eight years—and I'd like to see how many coppers Lydia squeezed out of her purse when it was talk of dad! So it was only right I should go and find out a bit from the old Baker. Mustn't fail dad now, if it was the last thing I did for him: I must hear how it happened. And the Baker would know—he helped carry him in. Must thank him for that. Only right I should go and thank him for what he done for dad. Least a man could do.

So I shut the gate behind me and found a fag-end in me pocket and lit it under the lamp. Then a car come creeping along by the wall with its sidelights on, as if it was looking for somebody. Just opposite me it stops; the door opens and the Baker himself looks out.

'Climb in, boy,' he says, and I climbs in because it was him I wanted to get hold of. 'I was over at your place,' he told me, 'and your sister said you'd gone to the churchyard. "I'll go there, then," I says, and she turned as red as a turkey-cock so I shoved off,' said the Baker.

I sat there in the front seat, and was I wild! Everybody knowed it was the Baker helped dad into nurse's house, so Lydia might a had the sense to say thank-you, at least. He switched on the headlights and the road lay there as white as a dance-floor. And off we went. It smelt good in that car, and the Baker had put stuff on his hair so it was like sitting in a barber's shop. Fine car. Smooth. Good as Nisse's any day. Only some folks always has to be best.

Drives well, there's no denying. Outside nurse's he brakes, throws out his right hand. Didn't say a word. Maybe he felt there was some things a man could understand without. So I looked out the window and seemed to see somebody lying there on the road, in front of Jacob's hedge. Imagination, of course. Just plain, silly imagination.

'We'll go home for a bit,' the Baker said, and stepped on it so the car jumped. Should I ask him about dad right away? Better leave it till we got there. He had to keep his mind on his driving and he might a got shirty if I bothered him now. There was that half-pint I had on me—I'd give it him, sort of thank you. I'd give it him when we got to his place. Ask him and thank him at the same time.

So we hadn't said a word when he pulled up at his own

gate. He must have thought I was a bit down over dad, so before we got out he clapped me on the shoulder.

'Chin up, boy,' he says.

So I grinned and got out. He'd done himself proud: new armchairs in the big room, and he'd got tiles on the old shack now, he said, instead of roofing-felt. Bought a radio-gram too—from town, he said. Not from that louse Nisse, then. Chairs was padded so soft you sank in up to your ears. He put on a record, so before a man could say anything we had to listen to it to the end. Only there was several, and it took a bit of time, and meanwhile the Baker put glasses on the table and took a bottle out of the cupboard. I couldn't do less, so I brought out my half-pint. The Baker goggled. 'Baker,' I said, 'Baker——' but there was no getting it out. There was no talking about dad. I should have to wait and warm up a bit first.

Up with me hand, now—up with it! When the Baker unscrewed the top and started pouring I made the stop sign. I didn't come here to drink. And if Lydia was sitting at home in the kitchen with the radio chap and Ulrik and the neighbour's girl saying 'Now Knut's drinking himself silly with that sot of a baker,'—well, let 'em. They'd always believed the worst of me. Just as if one couldn't be a decent man *and* a street-cleaner. But let 'em talk if they want to.

'What's the matter?' says the Baker. 'Not drinking your own *brännvin?*'

'Don't feel like it,' I tells him, but he says he'd be sorry if that was how I appreciated his hospitality. And I wouldn't want that. When you think what he done. After all, it was him took care of dad when dad fell off, so I drank to him all the same. Big glasses he had. So I wouldn't have more than one drink. Two at most.

He'd smartened the place up no end. Different from last time. He only had an iron bedstead then, and wooden chairs. Must see whether he remembers the ten he owes me. Shall I take and ask about dad? But there's that blasted gramophone that won't stop. I'll have to wait. His old woman's out, so for something to say I asks after her. But he gets mad. Tells me she's run away—not with anybody but back to her people in Medelpad. She went about saying that when he won on the pools all he did was drink, 'and one fine day—or night rather,' says the Baker, 'there was a note on the kitchen table. And not a scrap of food in the house. I was wild,' he says. 'So now I'm alone,' he says after a bit. And that great big fellow breaks down and cries. Looks at his hands and cries.

It's a shame. Good chap, the Baker. So I pours him out a drop, and one for meself too, so he shan't feel so miserable. That about dad'll have to wait; couldn't bother the Baker now. He's lying across the table howling. 'Chin up, boy,' I says. 'Haven't seen you since mum's funeral,' I says, 'so now we'll have a drink together.' To comfort him I takes another. Because he's a nice fellow.

'Took the dog with her too, she did,' he says. 'Enough to make anybody wild.' Well, that *was* a mean trick, to take the dog too; have to agree with him there. 'All right for you,' he says. 'Grieving for somebody who's dead, that's all right. But grieving for somebody who's alive, that's hell.' So I can't bring out anything about dad now—have to wait till he's calmed down a bit. Don't look hopeful, though, the way he's streaming at the eyes. 'We'll kill this bottle, then,' I says, to cheer him up, and empties the half-pint. To comfort him I knocks it back. It's a snorter. That'll have to do. I'm not tight, but I'm not going to give Lydia and her lot any handle against me.

85

But the old Baker won't be comforted, so it won't do to start on dad yet awhile. Instead I begin on Elinda: 'Don't you go thinking you're the only one who has trouble with his old woman.' And as soon as the talk turns on Elinda he brightens up. Not all at once, maybe. By fits and starts, like. So it seems that tale's known. He wipes his eyes, rubbing the palm of his hand over them. Draws the whisky cork too, but I says stop. That makes him miserable again, so—well, he can always pour it out. Drinking's another thing.

Hell of a long way inside me, though, that Elinda business. Worn me down long enough, it has, but just as bloody hard to bring out. So when the Baker wants to *skål* again I drinks with him. Well, I mean—no good sitting and stammering. Sounds as if a fellow was lying. After that it comes easier, and I must admit the Baker's helping me to drag it all out, so he must have known one or two things already. I got Lydia and Nisse to thank for that. So if they was to try and make trouble when I come home I'd have something to say to them, and that's a fact.

But it was a mess from the start. If Elinda had to go and find herself another man she could have found something better than that fat, pasty-faced swab from the market town. He'd been at school with Nisse and after I give him the treatment he went back there and talked. So there's a chap could do with another bashing if he was to turn up. Nisse too, so he couldn't drive round in his white shirt and gossip —not for the next six months. So I empties me glass and tells the Baker what really happened. In case he didn't know.

'I'd done eight months of my service,' I says, 'and we was to transfer from Jämtland to Linköping. So when we stopped in Stockholm on the way I slipped off home. A night with the old woman, I thought—just the job! So I took a taxi—sixteen crowns it come to, with the cleaning up—but worth it to sleep in a proper bed again. But when I come in the kitchen there was the fellow sitting on the settle with bare feet, and the wife on his knee darning his socks. So it didn't take me long to catch on. 'Take your socks,' I said, and snatched 'em from the wife, 'and then get out. You'll have at least one black eye before you're clear, I promise you that.' So the fellow pulls on his socks like a streak, and his shoes too—only then I saw they was me own shoes, so out he went in his stocking feet.'

The Baker just grins and eases out the cork. But that's enough, 'cause the bottle's waving about and the sweat pouring off me. So I makes the stop sign, but he just grins and goes on pouring. Pouring's one thing, drinking's another. There's such a thing as character, and that lot nattering at home can put that in their pipe and smoke it. 'Funny,' says the Baker. 'I heard different. Somebody said Nisse said it was you got beaten up.' Beaten up! Me! That's Nisse all over, the oily bastard. No, if anybody needs beating up, it's Nisse. I'll have a word or two with him when I get home. If I'm in good form, that is. When I got a few drinks on board I can say what I got to. Lot of hypocrites they are, that bunch at home. So I empties me glass and begins telling what really happened.

'I'd come straight from that Lapp dump, see? You ought to a been with us on that journey. We was ten fellows and ten quarts of *brännvin*, so you ought to a been with us. We was in cracking form when we got into town that night, and next day we was to go on to Linköping. So I took a taxi from Norra station home, and it come to twenty crowns with the cleaning up. So you can see, expense no object where the missus was concerned. What a happy surprise for her, I thought, and opened the door. And there the slut sits cuddling a fellow in the kitchen. Half-naked, he was, so it weren't hard to guess what they'd been up to. Now I always been good to my old woman as you know, Baker—you know me—so I just picked her up out of the way. But him, I snatched him off the settle. "Get your clothes on and do a round with me," I yells, and peels off me tunic, "You won't be winning no beauty contests after this," I tells him, quiet like, and out he flies—don't you make no mistake about that, boy. Out he flies, barefoot. I'm not one to pull me punches, you know that, Baker,' I says. 'So if anybody's running about blathering about me, they'll get it back, you know that, Baker,' I says. 'Maybe I ain't got so much padding in me shoulders as some, radio dealers for instance; but if they think that's where a man keeps his strength they're making a big mistake. Eight months I was, stuck in that Lapp dump, and not a woman the whole time. Just wait till I get back to the missus, I thought—twenty-five the taxi cost me. Not a penny more nor less, you know that, Baker,' I says. 'So you see, it was my old woman I was thinking of, first and last.'

Well, if there *are* tears in my eyes, the old Baker's not the fellow to mention it. Claps me on the shoulder he does, and says, 'Cheer up, Knut boy. You got friends, you know that, here if nowhere else.' 'You're all right, Baker,' I tells him. 'But I'd like to get me hands on some of that lot sitting at home slandering me.' And the Baker he says not to think about the wife. Nor I haven't, but when I do, how do I know what she's up to tonight? A chap's had a loss, he's in mourning, he's come down here to bury his old dad, and all the time his wife's out amusing herself. A chap's all alone. Not a damned soul he can trust. 'We'll knock this drop off,' says the Baker. My old woman needn't think she's the only one to have fun while I'm away in mourning. So we finishes off the drink.

'Eight months I was, in that Lapp dump,' I says. 'Yes, yes,' says the Baker, just as if he'd heard it all before. He needn't turn up his nose at me. Bigger chaps than him have had to climb down on my account. Lonely, I am, and nobody I can trust—not a perishing one—so no wonder I'm snivelling. 'Chin up, now, boy,' says the Baker. 'Let's go to the Pavilion.' So I tries to get up out of the chair, only you sinks so damn deep in the Baker's chairs. 'Hell of a way there,' I says. 'We'll never make it.' 'We'll go in the car,' says the Baker, and he grabs me arm, so I do get up at last. Only the floor's swaying like mad and down goes a glass when I grabs at the table. Silly idea putting glasses so near the edge. But the table's swaying too, so I hangs on to the radiogram—there's a vase there, and that's gone now. It was that last drink, I oughtn't to a took it. I was as clear as anything before that. Still, the wife needn't think she's the only one in the world to have a bit of fun.

'To hell with the vase,' says the old Baker. He puts out the light and we goes. So stuffy in that room I feel like throwing up—be better when I gets out in the air. Darn great stones in the path—trip me up so I fall on me knees. Annoying, that is; now the Baker'll think I'm drunk. Though he needn't turn up his nose. Rich he may be, but does he remember the ten he borrowed off of me? So I'll have one or two home truths to tell one or two people tonight. Nisse shall have a basinful some time, to remind him I'm not one to fool around with. And the iron-plater—if he's at the Pavilion, God help him.

Nice sitting in the car. And old Baker's a chap you can rely on. He's at the wheel, fiddling with the dashboard. Some knob he can't find, so we're not moving. Comical to see him squeezing the instrument-panel like it was a tart.

He must be good and tight. Chaps look as funny as hell when they're tight; so pardon the smile—well, the horse-laugh. I laughs so the door flies open and I nearly tumbles out. The Baker's getting really wild, and there isn't nothing funnier than a chap who's tight and wild as well. So I'm laughing fit to bust. At last he gets a noise out of it and we shoots backwards into an electric light pole. He starts babbling, then he stamps on the gas so we whizzes off like a cannon-ball. He can still drive, then! Cyclists yelling and shouting at us, and people standing by the roadside staring. He hasn't switched the lights on, either, so he can certainly drive. And me laughing till I cries, 'cause he's pretty tight.

Going that speed, there's the Pavilion in a few seconds. Lots of people there, staring at me because I'm laughing. As if a chap couldn't have a bit of fun now and then. There's a pothole by the entrance and I stumbles and falls on me knees. So now the doorman will think I'm tight. Sure enough, we're not getting in. The doorman's making the stop sign. 'What's this?' I asks, angrylike. 'What if it is a shoot-dinner —you don't have to shoot us!' Takes more than brass buttons to make me crawl. The Baker's no help, though. He grabs hold of me to keep me quiet and says to the doorman, sounding like he was worth fifty thousand at least, 'There are such things as newspapers.'

Always been quick, I have, so I catches on right away. 'Trust me,' says I. 'When I get back to town I'll write to the papers how shocking bad chucker-outs treats people in the country. A man could take that to any paper and get it printed,' I tells the doorman, but he only grins. So there's another I'll mark up when I get the chance. But the Baker's got me by the arm and we goes round the Pavilion and up into the wood and I trips over a root and the Baker gets wild and says, 'If you fall down again you can ruddy well lie there.' He needn't be so uppity. How can I help it if there's a root there?

There's just an ordinary fence round the Pavilion, with barbed wire along the top, so the Baker helps me and over I comes. I've caught meself on the wire, but nothing to speak of. We've fooled the doorman, and that's the main thing. Decent chap, that's what the old Baker is, and I takes him by the shoulder and tells him I'd been eight months in that Lapp dump. 'O.K., O.K.,' he says, giving me a shove—just as if I hadn't been talking of nothing else. He needn't think he can treat me like dirt. But he just walks on in spite of me shouting after him. He picks up a skirt by the open-air dance-floor and takes her out on it. But when I try, I get the brush-off. Money's what counts in this life, nothing else. Win on the pools first, then you can go dancing. Don't see anybody I know, but that don't bother me. Born and bred here, I was, but when you been twelve years in Stockholm you picks up a thing or two, so I walks about chatting to people. Nothing shy about me, and I can be damned good fun when I like. So I stops beside all the girls and talks to 'em, and you can see they think I'm good fun 'cause some of 'em's laughing fit to split. I'm no clodhopper any longer; I know how to handle skirts and nobody can't say different.

Then along comes the iron-plater. Drunk, he is, so I don't know what the doorman was thinking of to let him in. Good thing, though, 'cause now I can have a word with him. So I catches him by the collar and says, 'Now just you listen to me; if you think you can treat my dad so shabby you'll bloody-well have to think again.' 'Who the hell are you, throwing your weight about?' says the iron-plater. 'Knut Lindqvist, if that means anything to you,' I says. 'He was a decent old cove, was my dad, and I'll make you sorry you made him tight and sent him home like that.' I gets wilder and wilder, 'cause here's dad to be buried tomorrow, and the iron-plater's got no more respect than to go and get plastered the night before. 'A punch on the nose is what you're getting,' I tells him. But then somebody comes up and grabs my arm, and everybody standing round staring. But that don't do no harm, for at least they'll hear what sort of a bastard the iron-plater is. I spins round and there's the parish constable with his badge.

'We don't want any trouble from you, Lindqvist,' he says, the beggar. 'You go on home. You're burying your dad tomorrow, remember that.' I knowed what I could say to that, but up comes Baker with a popsy on his arm. 'Come along, Knut, we'll push off,' he says. 'I've got a half at home that we can finish.' A half! He must think I'm as tight as a tick, kidding me like that. Trying to protect the iron-plater, that's what it is. And if the flatfoot says I'm tight it's a damned lie, 'cause if I had a been I'd a fallen for the Baker's half-pint. But the constable's a hefty devil, for all he's old, and the iron-plater's hopped it. Scared, of course—but maybe he's hanging about outside, or running down the road. I'll ask the Baker to catch him up in the car, and then we'll see who gets the last word. Decent chap, the Baker, so he'll fix it.

So I'm going quietly, though the constable's walking behind, yammering and carrying on. Needn't think he's any dictator, though—by God he needn't. 'There is such things as newspapers,' I says to the Baker and his popsy. 'Yes, yes,' he says, just as if I hadn't been saying nothing else all the time. Can't get out quick enough to please the constable, though, 'cause he's walking behind thumping me on the back. 'Now then, Lindqvist' he says. 'Spelt with a qv, kindly remember,' I tells him—for he needn't think he can treat me like dirt. The doorman stares when we goes through the barrier. Must think he's seeing things, silly basket. 'There is such things as newspapers,' I tells him, and he looks scared. It works with yokels, threatening 'em with the papers.

Here's that blasted pothole. The Baker's bit will be thinking I'm tight. Quite a dish she is, too. I walk behind her and give her a pinch here and there, only the Baker says to give over. Can't carry his liquor, that's where it is. Otherwise he's all right. He climbs into the car and his piece beside him, and I crowds in front too. They thought I'd go in the back, but no fear—good fun sitting squeezed up to a girl, so when you gets the chance you takes it.

The Baker's going to show he can walk the white line all right. He comes smooth and slow on to the road with his lights on. Then he puts on the pace until the girl's bouncing. A nice bit she is, and it's not settled yet who's going to bed with her. I'm not much of a woman-chaser but I've always found it easy to get hold of girls. Eight months I was, in that Lapp dump, I tells her, but she only grins. 'Yes, yes,' says the Baker, stepping on it. 'Yes, yes!' Just as if I hadn't been talking of nothing else.

Stuffy all of a sudden, and the sweat pouring off me. Engine's made me go deaf. And the whisky up into me throat. Crack in the exhaust-pipe, must be, and the fumes coming into the car. But the old Baker don't say nothing. Blow me if the girl isn't stroking his chin! Stuffier and hotter all the time, and feels like somebody was pumping whisky up into me throat. And that blasted pudding they give me at home. And the road twisting all over the place—the wind catching the road and crumpling it and the fences rocking till I get seasick. I'm trying to wind down the window, but wrong handle and the door flies open.

'What the hell!' yells the Baker, slowing up. No need to yell. And he needn't think I'm going to let meself be treated like dirt by a bloody upstart like him—a fellow who can't even pay his debts of honour. But the fresh air's nice and the whisky's going down again. Near the nurse's place now. This is where the Baker come driving along that time. Ought to thank him—he done what was right. But the iron-plater—if I was to see him lying on the road I'd tell the Baker to drive over him. But he's slowing up and I'd better shut the door before he gets shirty. Must thank him, too, because this is the place.

'Baker,' I says, but it all comes up in me throat again. Gas must have got into the car and it's made me sick. 'Get out, damn you!' yells the Baker, and that's easy 'cause the door's open. So all of a sudden here I am on the road hearing the Baker blinding away inside: 'Spewing in my car, the swine. In my car——' The girl shuts the door and off they goes.

Not comfortable, the way I'm lying. Haven't broken anything, though, and I've got over the sickness. Only when I try to get up my legs is like clay. So I stay on me back and stretch out me hand and catch hold of a hedge—Jacob's hedge it is. Wonder if I'll get cold all at once. For it's dark at nurse's, and dark on the road, and not a single perishing star. Lonely, too, like I've always been. I remember very well at mum's funeral how everybody went round looking at me sideways. I've always been lonely. Dad was the only human one. And now dad's gone and here I am on me back in the road where dad had his last tumble, and if a car was to come along now God knows if it could stop in time. No wonder if I blubbers a bit. Cold, too. And it's starting to rain, so I'll get soaked through. Hell to go and get car-sick. Now they'll all be sitting in the kitchen at home, the whole ruddy gang, nattering

94

about Knut—how he'll have got drunk as usual. Can I help it if me legs is clay? Can I help getting car-sick? And that pudding—they can swallow that theirselves. There's a whole lot of things they can swallow. The inventory after mum's death and how Nisse took it home and fiddled it—they shall hear about that. It was only dad cared about a fellow, so is it any wonder a fellow cries? And I'm not drunk, because if you're drunk you ruddy well can't think about inventories— never could when I was tight. But now I'm clear in the head and they'd better watch out when I come home. Be worth getting after one or two of them. Measly old wreaths they bought—them as could afford better—but me in the street-cleaning, I wasn't so stingy. Stingy I've never been. And what do I get for it? Ingratitude. Who thanks me for going to the churchyard and putting eight crowns' worth of flowers on mum's grave? Or sending snuff-money regular to dad for eight long years? Twenty the taxi cost when I come from the Lapp dump, and a kick in the pants was what I got when I come home. My own wife helped to throw me out. Ingratitude all the way. No wonder a fellow's lying here on his back by Jacob's hedge and crying. There's a light at the bend. It's a car. Well, let 'em run over me. What's the odds? Then we'll see what they say, that mob in the kitchen at home— see if they don't take back one or two things they've said about me. Ah, at *that* funeral—they'll regret it, Lydia and her radio chap—they'll be sorry for what they done. And said. What a way to die. Car'll never stop in time, dark like this.

But when I been dead for a bit somebody shines a light in me face and shouts 'My God, it's Lindqvist's Knut. Tight as a tick. Can we lift him on to the bike and get him home? His dad's being buried tomorrow, so we can't leave him lying here in the road.'

So now they've found something to gossip about. They think I'm tight, though it's only I got clay in me legs. And so I tells 'em, now they got me on the carrier on me way home. That and a lot more. Eight months I was, in that Lapp dump, I tells 'em, so I seen a thing or two. Taxi from Norra station and the sod in the kitchen out like a shot. And the old woman's slippers after him. I'd a sent her too, only I know how to control meself. Eight months I was, in that Lapp dump, I says. 'Yes, yes,' says the fellow who's pushing—just as if I hadn't talked of nothing else. Think they can give 'emselves airs just 'cause a man's helpless for the moment. Can I help it if I'm car-sick? There's pills you can take for it, and I'll do that next time. Then there'll be no mistake. There's a chap holding me at the back like a constable and he won't have heard a word of what I been saying. So I turn me head and start: 'Eight months I was, in that Lapp dump,' but the silly devil tells me to pipe down. Just as if *he'd* been eight months in that Lapp dump. No good talking to these yokels. Wait till they come to town and has to go through what I had to go through.

Bumpy road, and they keep rocking the bike so I doze off. When I wake they've propped me against a fence, God knows what fence. Only now I can see we're home. So I follow the fence to the little gate; still a bit of clay in me legs, but I can hold up all right. Only I do fall over the steps—so darn dark. They might have lit the lamp, knowing a fellow was coming home. But nobody don't ever think about me. So I got to crawl all the way to the door and haul up by the handle. Hope nobody heard me trip over the steps, else I shall have to hear to my dying day that I was so tight the day before dad's funeral I couldn't stand on me legs. But no danger. They must all be asleep, this late.

Not on your life! When I open the kitchen door there they all are round the table, glaring at me like I was a ghost. Young Tage's come; he's drinking his coffee; got his uniform on. On the sarcastic side, one or two of 'em. Ulrik, for instance: 'So you been to the grave,' he says. 'Didn't fall in, I suppose, did you?' Then Lydia starts howling and won't stop. I'll go a bit nearer; still car-sick, I am, so it seems to me I can be forgiven for not going straight to the right chair. Anyhow I don't go to any chair, but over to the sink, for the neighbour's girl's washing up. And she's sweet, she is, if she is a bit countrified, and I'd put an arm round her only she starts howling too. So God knows what they been saying about me while I was in the churchyard. 'Leave the girl alone,' says the radio chap, pompouslike. And Lydia blubbering like a lunatic. 'Just look at him,' she keeps on. 'All over sick and filth from head to foot. And a tear in the seat of his trousers. And no hat. And too drunk to stand up.'

How could I know there was a chair behind me? I trips over it when I turns. That could happen to anybody. And sheer insults—that I won't take. Oh they can get on their high horse, but buy flowers for mum's grave—that's beyond 'em. And too much to expect 'em to be interested enough about dad to go and ask the person who helped carry him in to nurse's how it all happened.

So I goes up to the table and bangs me fist on it so Tage's cup falls on the floor, and lets 'em hear a few home truths. 'For eight months I sent snuff-money to dad,' I tell 'em, 'and I wonder which one of you has done more. And mum got clothes from Elinda till her dying day. One or two of you finds it hard to stomach me being in the street-cleaning, as I well know. Dirtying things is easy enough, though, *I* say— sweeping up's a sight harder.'

D   97

But they're so cussed the lot of 'em that they start sounding off about me suit, just as if the best suit I've got ain't good enough for a country funeral. 'Shut up, you,' I says. ' 'Tisn't everybody lives by cheating people with old radio sets and can afford to buy a white shirt every other day. There may not be much pickings in the cleaning business, but I'll be damned if I'm ashamed of my trade.'

But what's the use? Here I stand saying what I has to say to my family, not to mention other odds and sods present, but nobody's listening. Makes you boil. Lonely, I am—always have been. Can't wonder a fellow's snivelling a bit. 'He can have my suit,' says Tage. 'I got me uniform for the funeral.' And that blasted radio chap says Tage's clothes will fit all right, if Tage ain't afraid of having 'em sicked up over. So I says to the old carcase that anybody can get car-sick if they're not used to it, and it weren't everybody could lounge about in a Volvo 39 or whatever it was, every day of his life. 'Pontiac', he says, 'and they'll fit', he says, 'for he's got the build of a rooky, for all he's thirty-three'. But like I tell him, a man don't have to be as fat as some people to give 'em a poke in the jaw. If need be. And him—to think what he comes out with: 'Then you better start with Elinda's boy-friend, before they eats you out of house and home.'

I'm alone by the table. I've had a loss, I'm in mourning. While the wife crawls into bed with somebody else. And a fellow's own brother and sister not listening for half a second to what he's got to say. How people do let you down. Lonely —always have been. And so I'm snivelling. Why not, when Lydia's at it as hard as she can? Only at last she comes up to me and says 'Go to bed'. Quite worn out she must be, 'cause I has to steady her all the way into the bedroom. And the bedroom's as stuffy as hell, so the car-sickness starts again.

Have time to throw meself on dad's couch, though, before it comes. Only it don't come, because self-control's one thing I *have* learnt. Only by rights I ought to get up and pee. But Lydia's turned bossy. 'Lie still,' she snaps, and begins pulling off me trousers. So I shall hear to my dying day that Knut was so drunk before dad's funeral that his sister had to pull off his pants. Jacket too. Treating me like a shop-window dummy. But Lydia and her radio chap needn't think they can do as they like with me, and so I tell Lydia and she begins snivelling again and calling me a liar 'cause I haven't never been to mum's grave with the flowers. I have though, and raked it too, I tell her, for she couldn't know that. But then she loses her temper properly and tugs me arm till it nearly comes out of joint. 'You're drunk and you're lying,' Lydia says, ' 'cause the family grave's opened up for dad, so there wasn't nothing to rake when Nisse and me was there dinnertime.'

So I been and put the flowers on the wrong grave. And if they're not there tomorrow that's eight crowns down the drain. And me branded as a liar into the bargain. And ill. And back in town me own wife in bed with somebody else. And Yngve, the boy who runs and hides whenever I come home. So there's been backbiting everywhere, and is it any wonder I snivel, lying here nearly naked on dad's couch and snivelling. Dad's lain here many a time. And here we sat, dad and me, the last time we saw each other. So there, Lydia— dad was fond of me, at any rate. And when we was sitting here together on the couch he got up and went over to the chest of drawers and pulled out a drawer and hunted through it. And after a bit he found what he wanted and laid it on the table. It was a little jersey. 'Remember this, Knut?' said dad. 'Remember the Iceland jersey? I bought it in town one

99

Christmas Eve and you was as pleased as Punch with it,' said dad. So I could do with that Iceland jersey now. Dad had it in his hands last time I was here. I could do with it, to hold in my hands under the blanket and think about dad with.

So 'where's my Iceland jersey?' I asks Lydia. Lydia's standing by the couch. Lydia's nose looks like a thumb on a copper saucepan. Her face is so red it's shining. 'Where's my Iceland jersey?' I asks, but she don't answer. Thinks I'm raving, of course. Only then she says, 'Your Iceland jersey! Going to wear it to the funeral, I suppose, instead of your suit. The suit can go to a pensioner at the workhouse.' So Lydia don't understand—not one bit. And I can't start looking for it myself, 'cause as soon as I raise my head I get a throatful. Car-sickness is hell.

Lydia's standing with my jacket over her arm, staring at it as if it done her some harm. 'And you've lost your crape band,' she says.

My crape band. That's turned me cold. I've stopped being angry. Stop feeling ill-used. Forget all about Elinda. Not crying any more now over being so good-hearted. I'm lying on dad's couch seeing what a swine I am. Losing the mourning-band's like losing the sorrow. I stepped off the straight and narrow and just let it slip off me arm—that's how much I've been thinking of dad: losing my crape band on a blind. A fellow's a swine—always has been and always will. I shut me eyes not to see it all, but it's there just the same. The crape band must be lying in the spew in the car, or hanging on the barbed wire round the Pavilion, or maybe somebody'll find it by the dance-floor and say 'Here's a crape arm-band some-body's lost. That'll be Knut, of course—that sot who can't even keep sober for his dad's funeral. And when his mum was buried it was just the same. So that Knut Lindqvist, he's a

brute, a filthy brute. "Spelt qv" he said to the constable, so
he's put on airs since he went and turned street-sweeper in
town.'

And now as I sink down into something disgustingly
yellow and warm I remember all in a lump how it was at
mum's funeral. That morning I had to throw up out the
window, and Ulrik was going by with the milk-pails and that
sneer on his face. 'I'll let you off mopping up the ground,'
he said, 'but by God you'll clean up the lobby floor.' And next
time I woke I hadn't no trousers on 'cause I'd caught 'em on
a gate when I was tight and torn the knee. Lydia was mending
'em in the kitchen. Later I sneaked down to the cellar and
took a hefty nip. On an empty stomach, so it showed. I'd
a had to walk to the car alone, only for dad: he took me by
the arm. I was drink-sick and then I got car-sick, so we got
to the church at the last minute. Damned slow they drove.
And in the cellar Nisse and Ulrik unscrewed the lid and there
was mum, yellow and thin, and she had a pointed nose, and
Ulrik put back the handkerchief and I was holding the candle
and crying and the tears nearly put it out. And the squeak
when they screwed the lid on for the last time. And the verger
went first and us after him with the coffin. I took the foot-end.
'You're the puny one,' Ulrik said, and it's true I didn't look
much in that suit. So I come last. Church was full of people,
all staring—old 'uns, mostly. It was July and the sweat
pouring down, so I was glad enough to set the coffin down in
front of the altar. After that I just held my handkerchief over
my face the whole time and the earth from the pastor's trowel
sounded like a rattlesnake. Then it was up and carry again,
me shoulder hurting so I could a screamed. I was nervous
and got the straps mixed, and Nisse wanted to say something,
you could see, only then he remembered he was in church so

he saved it. Slow back to the mortuary feeling like death. And mum smelling a bit—ever such a tiny bit—but maybe it was only me noticed it. Then we lowered it into the grave and being limp I let go too soon, so without the others was stronger there'd a been a crash. I'd have liked to speak but all I could do was snivel and drop the wreath. And then back to the cars and the funeral dinner. Lydia whispered I'd brought too much *brännvin* with me and the old fellows was beginning to get drunk, and I said that mum ought to a been with us 'cause it would a made her damned happy to see us all so damned happy. Said it aloud, and the looks I got from the family would a turned the milk. But dad he thought the same; he sat there getting tighter and tighter, and I was glad. For dad didn't always have such a good time of it, either. And in the evening we sat in his room together, and that I'll never forget.

And as I'm sinking now I know it'll be the same story tomorrow. Only not the same. For now there's no dad to take a man into his room and talk to him like a human being. Nobody left who isn't sly and deceitful. Tomorrow I shall be alone. All alone. Who could wonder at me crying, lying here in this room, undressed by me own sister, sinking into a drunken sleep? Who could wonder a man should want to have his old Iceland jersey to stroke under the blanket?

'Where's my Iceland jersey?' I asks Lydia; but it's too late, for now, next minute, me nose is under and I don't hear another thing. Still, just for a second I'm still alive. 'Beast,' I hear Lydia say. Quiet but very clear. And a cuckoo calling, somewhere high in the air. Dad's clock's going again.

OPEN

THE

DOOR,

RICHARD

Open the door, Richard!

OPEN the door. . .

They were telling me to open the door, and I wouldn't. They didn't just tell me, they begged me, and when begging was no good they threatened, and when threats didn't work they kept quiet for a bit; they whispered breathlessly, eagerly, standing absolutely still outside the door as if they wanted to hypnotise it. Or perhaps hypnotise me through the keyhole. Hyp-no-tise. . . .

But I wouldn't open it. And not only that—I retreated further and further into the room, as far as I could get—as far as the bed in the corner. I lay down on that bed and covered my head with the pillow, so as not to hear, not to see, not to know. And yet sometimes I do know—the thing I have to know forces its way in to me along infernal channels which it would take all the pillows in the world to block. I had only one—a good pillow, thick, close and soft—but what good was that, now!

What good. No good at all, and yet there are moments in this locked room when all torment suddenly ceases, when the pillow is enough, and a calm joy—sweet as honey—flows into me. At such moments I am open; I see myself as an ocean receiving a broad, gentle river in its arms, and allowing itself to be kissed into warmth and happiness by its mild waters. At these rare moments I can even release myself from the pillow, let it fall off the bed, and with my neck resting on my clasped hands look the ceiling above me in the eye. Then it's not just a locked door that separates me from the people out there—not just a long, narrow room full of silence—but something much stronger, much more ruthless in its power to isolate.

But something had happened outside, for suddenly someone—either Knut or Inge—took a hard step towards the door
and began knocking on it with his knuckles, and although the
person knocking wasn't altogether sober, yet there was dia-
bolical calculation in that knock. It didn't attack first one
part of the door and then another, but concentrated on one
spot just above the handle, and applied itself to it with as
calm and terrible an obstinacy as if it meant to pierce a hole
through the door and so compel me.

Let them keep on, I thought jubilantly—let them break
their knuckles, bash their hands until they bleed. God, how
wrong they are if they think they can make me turn the key
before I choose.

So for the moment I could leave the pillow where it was;
for the moment it almost tickled me that anyone should wear
out his knuckles on my account. I stretched myself out on
my bed; I was on holiday. I knew it wouldn't last long. This
wasn't the first time it had happened, and so I knew it wouldn't
last long. Soon enough I should find that whoever was
knocking wasn't knocking at the cold, insensible door but
on my warm, aching body. Knuckles always know what they
want—knuckles always know where it hurts most—knuckles
are so used to my body that they find the most sensitive spots
unaided.

Then the knocking stopped for an instant, and Knut
whispered (so it was he who had been knocking),

'Open up, my sweet—come now, my sweet, open up,
open up!'

Then there was silence; silence outside the door, that is;
and because it was so quiet outside the door I could hear the
cracked, drunken voices in the kitchen. Women there, too.
I knew they'd brought women with them, but not even that

touched me now. As long as I had the strength not to open the door, nothing could touch me.

Now I heard them muttering again outside. I was proud and happy enough not to strain my ears to catch what they were saying about me. I knew they were baffled, I knew I had the upper hand. They couldn't do anything to me as long as the kitchen was full of their tipsy friends. A husband can't tell a drunken friend that his wife has 'locked herself in and won't come out, the witch'. If he did the friend would laugh, and every scrap of that laughter would pierce the husband's soul like a bomb-splinter. He'd lose face, and face is a drunk's most precious possession—and not only a drunk's, but an ordinary man's too. A man's face is like a doorhandle: even if it's on the door of a hovel it must look like the door-handle of a bank or a tavern. It must always look proud, brassy proud, and the woman's task is to polish forth this pride from beneath the patches of cowardice and despair.

Knut wouldn't shout about it, for what man wants others to know that he's got a dotty wife? And Inge wouldn't bash the door in, for what man wants people to know that he's got a mad sister? So they stood there debating the point, and so far they were too sober to agree on any plan. Someone was screaming in the kitchen; I'm sure it was a woman, but don't imagine I cared about that. I was lying here without a pillow, noting the scream—a sharp, female little scream. Playful.

'Come on now, my sweet,' said Knut as I smiled at the ceiling, 'my darling sweet, why won't you open the door? Are you angry with me? What have I done? You might at least tell me what I've done.'

Done. . . .

Knut, my dear, I thought—or so I thought I thought— Knut, my dear, you haven't done anything. A normal person wouldn't think you'd done anything. A normal person would think you were a pretty decent type. But I can't be normal. A normal person wouldn't have shut herself into a room and lain there sulking just because her husband's come home from work some hours later than he usually does on Saturdays, bringing a couple of wet friends and their wives or girls— or some sort of girls—back with him.

And yet this is what had happened. Just this. When I'd heard them on the stairs, laughing, filling the whole staircase with a stream of raucous voices, I turned out the gas, threw my apron over the back of a chair, ran into my room and turned the key. Then I stood close against the door and heard them fussing into the hall and fussing into the kitchen. And I heard low, ambiguous laughter from the women as they sat down on somebody's knee. I supposed that drink was appearing on the table, and coffee-cups, and that one of the cups was broken by somebody. Knut talked big and shouted what the hell did it matter.

But then quite plainly I heard him beginning to shrink, especially after he'd shut the kitchen door and was standing alone, coughing with embarrassment, in the hall. I couldn't see him, of course, but I knew what he was looking like and how he would behave. He was looking angry and ashamed— perhaps chiefly ashamed, for a man ought not to come home after a day's work and find his wife missing. One's wife must be in her proper place, especially on a Saturday; she must be as unfailingly present as the pint-bottle in the kitchen cupboard.

Knut began hunting. He opened the door of the WC, and although it was probably quite unnecessary he went in and stayed there for a while: one mustn't let on that one's looking for one's wife. I stood close against the door, listening to the play-acting—for play-acting it was: he knew perfectly well that I'd locked myself in here. It wasn't the first time, but it was the first time he'd had to bother about it. The other times he had come home on his own, or else we'd been sitting alone together in the kitchen and suddenly I sprang up and ran into the bedroom and locked the door. Then he'd waited for a bit, walked up and down a few times between the stove and the door, lit a pipe and then rung up my brother and arranged to meet him outside a tavern. At those times he won by going—by leaving me alone instead of trying to come in.

Was that what I wanted? Is that what I want? Doesn't one lock oneself into a room in order to be alone? No, not I. The first time, when Knut stayed out all night with Inge, he found me crying on the mat in the bedroom with my head wrapped in a drenched pillowslip. And he lay down on the bed in his shoes, shouting that he was the world's most considerate husband to leave his confounded wife in peace when she wanted to be alone.

Alone. Alonalonalonal. . . .

Lonal onal onal. . . .

Once, though, he came and knocked, and at first I let him knock. Then I let him plead for a time. Surely I may be forgiven that little scrap of contrariness. I only wanted to teach him what it was like to have to fight a bit to get a woman. I only wanted him to help me conquer my loneliness by breaking in on it. While he was pleading I undressed without a sound, and when I turned the key I was almost naked. And yet he never saw me. He walked straight into the room with the hasty indifference of one walking into a telephone box. He pulled out a drawer of his writing-table, took a pint-bottle that was lying in it and disappeared for the whole evening. I could have sunk through the floor in my nakedness. I felt like a slighted prostitute, and no wonder.

But tonight it was different. I stood listening to Knut's steps, and the way they reluctantly, timidly and tipsily approached the bedroom door, the nearer the more slowly, because they knew. And then the handle that was pressed gently down and the curse that didn't come, because he knew.

'Inge', he shouted through the kitchen door. 'Here a minute. You're wanted on the telephone.'

Inge's my brother, but not only my brother. He's much more than that: he's Knut's conscience. It's difficult for a man's conscience to neglect his wife as much as he'd like to. Inge is a good thing for Knut to have. Inge's purpose is to make him think: 'Well, sometimes I do go out and don't come home, but at least it's her brother I'm with. Her brother, mind you!'

There are no words as good as 'at least'; I know them. I know they can be used as a pole to push someone else deeper into the mire.

But Inge came. Inge's no fool, and he understood at once what had happened. Inge, I thought as I stood by the door, at least you're my brother. I'm relying on you. Help me to get out of here without having to forfeit myself. I was on the point of saying this to him, but if I had, I would have bitten my tongue through a few seconds later. For this is what Inge said to Knut.

'What d'you want with her when you *have* got her out? Let her sulk if she wants to. Some women enjoy it. Leave her alone until she softens up.'

That was when I felt I needed a pillow. That was when I crawled over to the bed. Perhaps I didn't exactly crawl, though that's what it felt like. It seemed to me that a whole gallery of gay, tipsy, merciless eyes was watching my brief flight across the floor from the door to the bed, and it was they who made me crawl, though in fact I may have run. Drowned in a pillow I heard the two outside going away, and then almost immediately coming back.

They're coming back, I thought, although the pillow was there to stop me thinking. They're coming back. So they've left something in here. There's something in here they want. Or——

I got up and searched the room, pulled out drawers, opened cupboard doors, looked under clothes and behind china, but there was no drink hidden anywhere. I needed the pillow again for a moment to cover my doubt with. I mustn't be weak, I thought. Only once does a woman open the door to a man in vain. As they stood there pleading, afraid of being heard by the roaring people in the kitchen and afraid of not being heard by me, I lay with a pillow pressed hard about my head to stifle my foolish desire to spring up and turn the key and show my stupid, happy face to the two men outside. But pain sneaked in under the pillow and drove the aching into me, reminding me of that frightful moment of humiliation; yet joy clung to the pain like a leech, and the leech sucked out my pain and I became happy and weak enough to let the pillow fall.

I'm coming, I thought. I'll open the door. I know now that it's on my account you're knocking. You've got all you want in the kitchen: drink and women and laughing men. And yet you're standing there. You need me too. Another minute and I'll come.

When one has been very lonely, nothing is so precious as the moments before the end of loneliness, and I put off what I was going to do because it made me richer. Each lonely minute pumped me fuller of happiness. I was a toad and the toad was thinking, 'My skin will still stretch. Plenty of time before it splits.'

And then suddenly it was too late. If the kitchen door hadn't opened at just that moment I'm certain I'd have been on my way to my own door. But the kitchen door did open, and I was still lying on my bed, distended and motionless with happiness, like a snake that has swallowed a rabbit. A woman came out first, and then they all came. And the men who had been waiting for me stopped coaxing. Suddenly they weren't waiting for me any longer; they were simply waiting for their dignity to catch up with them. At last it did, and Inge cried,

'We're trying to coax my sister out, but it won't work.'

And Knut cried,

'Well, are you coming or aren't you!'

And then I couldn't come. I was paralysed and just lay there, and one hand dropped down off the bed and began groping for a pillow. But before the hand found it, one of the unknown women out there began to sing. If you could call it singing. I was too tired and too far away.

'Open the door, Richard. Open the door and let me in.'

I ought to have jumped up then and shrieked at the top of my voice: 'My name isn't Richard. I'm not a man, and above all I'm not a whore with time to run in and out of music-shops all day, looking for gramophone records for my customers!'

I ought to have—but I didn't. Instead I pulled the merciful pillow over my head, and now it was like dough, finding its way into all the cracks in my face, sealing them and stiffening there. Everything that happened after that I could hear and grasp, but I couldn't do a thing about it. I couldn't even make my face twitch for sorrow.

And when the hall door had slammed and the whole party were carrying their echoing bursts of laughter down the stairs I couldn't even reflect, 'Our windows ought to overlook the street—anyhow not the courtyard, for not a soul comes into the courtyard on Saturday afternoons.' No, I just lay there, and the pillow grew and grew—it became roof and walls and floor. Yet that wasn't what I feared. It was the terrible awakening that I dreaded, which no art of mine could postpone. I should become small and ordinary again. I should get up and go to the door and unlock it and walk into the kitchen and drink a glass of water. Then I should go back and lie down on the bed in my unlocked room and think only of one thing before I fell asleep—if I did fall asleep: It's only when I'm alone that I can unlock the door. Only when there's nobody to come in can I leave my door open. How lonely must I make myself before at last somebody discovers my loneliness and saves me? Breaks into my room?

MEN

OF

CHARACTER

Men of Character

CROWN foresters wear puttees, either grey or green. This one was always in a hurry and half-ran through the village, the dust flying about his ankles. Everybody greeted him, but he greeted none, perhaps because he was in such desperate haste that he had no time to see those he met, though they always slackened speed and made way when they saw him coming. Sometimes they stopped right by the ditch and turned their heads as he passed, imagining that he had a dog on a leash: a big, invisible dog to which he whistled silently and adapted his stride, and by which his attention was too much engaged to be caught by anything else. People nudged each other but never laughed—never even smiled; they only showed by their look that they were thinking about that dog.

He took the concrete steps of Cederblom, Grocer, in two leaps, and old women who had been standing at the foot of them offering each other snuff started aside in a fright. When he entered the shop he unslung his gun, stood with his feet wide apart on the newly-scrubbed boards and weighed the weapon by the sling until he found the point of balance. Only then did he step forward to the counter, and all the eyes that had been staring at him with curiosity or bewilderment slewed hastily away. When the gun was resting with its butt on the floor the barrel stuck up an inch or two above the top of the counter, and the two women shop-assistants looked scared as they placed paper bags and cartons in front of their customers. When his turn came he handed the girl a type-written sheet, and not even when she told him that something or other was out of stock was he heard to utter a word.

He simply shook his head disapprovingly and shrugged his shoulders, as if to rid himself of displeasure at the news. He always bought the same things: provisions for his expeditions into the woods. Tinned food, hard bread, goat's cheese, oranges, coffee and condensed cream, or essentially masculine goods associated with strength, solitude and superiority: puttees, boot-grease of an exclusive brand, expensive pipe-tobacco, good pipe-cleaners, pocket-flasks for field use or flints for cigar-lighters. When the goods were ranged before him on the counter he packed them into his rucksack himself, the abruptness of his movements preventing the shop-assistant from helping him. Nobody in the village had ever heard him ask for help, and so nobody had ever heard him say thank you either. Nobody had ever seen his match blow out when he lit his pipe in the wind, or heard him swear because he had a stone in his shoe. The things that make other people look ridiculous never happened to the forester—nothing that one could laugh at or smile about. But one never knew. . . .

One day the forester came into the shop and bought a headscarf. For once he had left his gun and rucksack at home, and he wore no gloves; there was general surprise that his hands were so small—so small and so white, almost like a woman's. He was smoking a cigarette that looked absurdly tiny in the middle of that great red face. From the moment he entered Cederblom's he behaved strangely; he went not to the big counter but to the little glass one to the left in the passage-way, where there were things that the villagers used to look and giggle at, but never buy: cheap necklaces, brightly-coloured bathing-wraps, mascots, gay silk bathing-dresses (to be worn where, among these woods?) cigarette-holders and ear-rings. Over this museum of urban vanity the forester leaned for some time, puffing vigorously at his cigarette without taking it from his mouth, before any assistant had the presence of mind to go up to him.

When in an amiable though somewhat awkward voice he said he wanted a cloth, the girl misunderstood him, and began spreading table-cloths and runners over the counter.

'Not that kind,' said the forester, spitting out his cigarette and grinding it under his boot. 'I mean to wear round the head.'

'You mean for warmth?' asked the assistant, who naturally didn't gather it was to be for a lady, and remembered having seen people with toothache wearing white cloths round their heads.

Then the forester looked down into the glass case as into an aquarium, and at last discovered what he was looking for. He walked round the counter, which extended some way across the floor, and pulled out the drawer of headscarves. Picking up the first that came to hand, he looked for a second at the fiery red, transparent silk, and in a low, rapid voice asked the girl to wrap it up for him. Then he slipped the little parcel into the pocket of his shooting-coat and stood for a moment on the steps outside, trying to light a cigarette in the rain. Through the shop-window the assistant saw him hurrying on along the road, his lips closed on the cigarette like a vice. Just before the bend he stopped suddenly, took one of his delicate hands from his pocket and stretched it out in the rain, as if tasting it. But he went on again at once and was soon out of sight even from the further window of the shop. He had looked queer, though. Very queer.

By the evening nearly everybody knew about the forester's headscarf, and many people talked about it after they'd put the light out and lay with the cat on the blanket, listening to the cars along the road and waiting to fall asleep. Next morning the schoolmaster's wife came bicycling to Cederblom's as usual. Her name was Alice and she was the daughter of a farmer in the neighbouring parish. The weather was clear; it was warming up after the rain, and the shop door was open. On the threshold she turned and went back to her bicycle as if she had forgotten something; she fiddled with the padlock and tool-bag, and when she came up the steps again her head was bare. Yet as she went over to the counter she realised that it was too late. The little knot of women who stood fingering a bale of dress-material followed her with their eyes all the way across the floor; she knew that they might have seen her through the window wearing the forester's headscarf and would then realise that she'd been cowardly and put it in her shopping-bag. This made the bag feel so heavy that she could hardly carry it, and the shop-assistants look made it heavier still. She blushed deeply, and when she began to give her order she couldn't remember a single thing she meant to buy; but not wanting to admit her confusion, even to herself, she asked for a number of unnecessary things, including a pair of cuff-links—a very thoughtless purchase, as she realised as soon as she had mentioned them, and doubly so as the women were still in the shop. But it would have looked silly to change her mind. When the assistant opened her bag to help her put in her purchases, she hated him for taking out the scarf in front of everybody and laying it on the counter, as he remarked acidly that it was a shame to put all the heavy parcels on top of such a pretty scarf.

By midday the forester—who rented an upstairs room in the schoolmaster's house—and the schoolmaster's wife were encircled; widely and at a distance, it's true, but there were many to hold the net and chances of escape were slight indeed.

One oughtn't to pay attention to what children say, never-theless children are dangerous because they haven't the sense to conceal the truth. Through the half-open classroom door the schoolmaster heard one girl chasing another along the corridor, and was just going to speak to them when one was evidently overtaken, for she stopped abruptly just outside, not knowing that he was still there.

'Who?' shouted the girl who had been chasing her, in a voice harsh with excitement. 'Who? Who? Who-who-who?'

'The forester,' panted the other, and she ran off laughing—ran out pursued by the other, leaving the schoolmaster alone with his thoughts and his shame, his hot, quivering unease, his sweet, titillating pain. When the class came in he was sitting red-faced at his desk. Or so he felt. He had to look down at himself too, to convince his uneasy self that he wasn't naked. He buttoned his jacket, although the weather was as hot as midsummer, and pulled up the zip-fastener of his sports shirt to the chin. In contrast to his usual manner he questioned the pupils abruptly and nervously, and gave the answers himself if they were too slow about it. He avoided the two girls and dared not even look in their direction.

When he arrived home that afternoon he heard the forester pacing to and fro upstairs in his room, but he gave no sign of this and tried to seem pleasantly unconcerned, though he really wanted to have the matter out. From this moment, perhaps almost against his will, he began to collect material for a showdown. There is no better tracking-dog, no more resourceful detective, no more ruthless hunter than a jealous husband. At one school-break he borrowed a colleague's bicycle and told the class he had to go to the station to send an urgent telegram, so that he might be a few minutes late for the next lesson. Once out on the road he did in fact start off in the direction of the station, but soon, when he was alone on the road, he turned warily and took a track through the woods. He rode fast and the machine jolted over roots and stones. He wanted to take his house by surprise, in the rear, and a few hundred yards from the back gate he braked, propped the bicycle against a tree and went the last bit of the way on foot. He stole behind a bush and lit a cigarette, to stiffen his dignity in an undignified situation. The gate was freshly oiled and didn't squeak, and he entered stealthily, on tiptoe through the grass. Through the twitter of birds and the snap of the flag-halliard he heard low voices coming from the arbour, and he drew clouds of smoke into his mouth as he peered in through the little newly clipped entrance.

There they lay on the grass, although there was a table to sit at. True, they were only drinking coffee and had the coffee-pot and the plate of cakes between them, but his wife was wearing a gay headscarf which he didn't recognise; she was smoking, which was not a habit of hers, and sometimes they spoke so softly that he couldn't hear what they were saying, though he tried hard enough.

But school breaks are short—shorter than one thinks when one has sneaked away on a bicycle—and before his cigarette was finished the schoolmaster walked up to the house, flung open the door loudly enough to be heard, and stamped on the threshold as if he had snow on his shoes. He was standing in front of the hall looking-glass, blowing smoke at his insipid reflection to impress it, when he heard his wife running up the verandah steps. She saw him the moment she came in, and stopped short. Her head was bare.

'I thought I heard a noise in the house,' she said. 'It was you, then.'

'It was,' he said, and went. He tossed his cigarette end on

to the floor for her to tread out. Slouched down the front steps. Whistled as he passed the arbour, which lay quite silent in the heat—no, the forester was putting cups and saucers together and clearing his throat. As the schoolmaster was riding back through the woods he met at a bend in the path a sweaty little woman gathering fir-cones in a sack. She was the mother of one of the little girls who knew the Truth. When he pedalled past he could see that she was going to ponder over this odd encounter in the woods, in school hours. It was a nuisance, but unavoidable.

His wife went into the kitchen for the dustpan and brush and swept up the tobacco-ash. She drank a glass or two of water and wandered about the ground floor opening windows to catch a breath of air. She was glad of the wind, and leaned out of the big bedroom window to let it fan away her sudden anxiety. But the solace was a brief one. A network of merciless little meshes seemed to be drawing close about her body, and she had to thrust her hand inside her frock and pass her fingers over her skin to convince herself that it was pure imagination. She would have liked to run away somewhere, but in some direction that didn't exist: not to the arbour, nor Cederblom's, nor the road, nor the school, nor the woods.

Someone was coming through the gate from the woods; the latch had clicked beyond the arbour. A woman was walking over the lawn dragging a sack over the grass. She passed close, close by the arbour, and the woman standing in the window bit her lip and hoped that the man in there wouldn't call to her or come rushing out to grab her and crush her to himself, as was his way when they were alone. The schoolmaster's wife went out and met the woman with the sack just by the verandah steps. The woman stopped then, dropped the sack on the stones of the path and pushed her hair back from her sweaty forehead. Then she looked the schoolmaster's wife in the eyes with an expression that was hard to interpret: it was neither benevolent nor malicious. Yet the wife felt a little at a loss and found nothing to say; she just looked down at the sack and then past it, towards the arbour. Then she saw that Fru Mattsson was beginning to look in the same direction, and so as not to betray herself she diverted the other's gaze and moistened her tongue to ask why she had come. But the peasant-woman forestalled her.

'Do you mind me crossing your land,' she said with a question that was no question, and lifted her sack. 'The sack's heavy, see, and this is a bit of a short cut.'

It sounded all right, and would have sounded even better if she had kept her eyes still; but they wavered and shifted into the house and out again, up to the forester's window and down the garden between the apple-trees then hovered for a moment like hawks above the arbour. It was as if she could see into it, although she stood on the stones at Alice's side, breathing heavily after her exertions.

'Of course, Fru Mattsson,' said Alice at last, and she took hold of the sack.

But Fru Mattsson wanted no help. The offer made her suspicious and she found excuses to linger in front of the verandah. There were invisible cats to stroke, flowers to admire and scents to inhale as she sent her eyes straying over the house and garden.

'A nice home you've got,' she said, looking the schoolmaster's wife in the eyes for the last time, and moved off. They were queer, the people here—they said neither good morning nor goodbye. They looked insolent when they came and stared insolently when they left. She plodded away with her sack, but just as she was opening the gate on to the road the thing she'd been waiting for happened: the forester called out.

'Alice, where the hell have you got to?'

It was as if Alice were hearing his voice for the first time, and she stiffened where she stood. An eternity passed before the gate clicked again. The click roused her, and she rushed on to the verandah, into the hall, upstairs and into her room, the door of which stood wide open. She locked it and dropped into an armchair, and at first when the forester knocked she didn't open to him. When at last she did he was standing outside, his hands busy with pipe and tobacco-pouch, uncomprehending.

'What the hell's got into you?' was all he said.

She was suddenly enraged. Such denseness was intolerable. Being new to the situation she found it utterly beyond her control. The fear which throughout the spring had been dammed up by renewed caresses, fresh secret joys, forced its way out in a long scream—a long outburst of shame and dread. She had believed she knew what it was to defy the world, but she had really only toyed with the idea of ultimate discovery. She had let such thoughts leap skywards like rockets and buried her head in his flesh to enjoy their perilous, dazzling brilliance. The curtains in his room had always been drawn for a few hours of the day, for them to pretend that it was night. They had strengthened each other by seeking mutual protection. She had crept into him as into a cave, and in the warmth and soft dimness the hostile outer world had seemed absurdly, ludicrously impotent. The long intervals between the brief moments in the forester's room had been like a bridge between glorious islands which helped her awareness of the alluring, strengthening bond with her lover—a bridge of memories: memories of a finger-tip on a breast, a bite in a shoulder, a kiss on the throat, a warm hand gliding down a back.

Fear of discovery had been only a game, because not for an instant had she been alone—until now, when she knew suddenly that discovery itself would make her lonely, so terribly lonely that nothing could defend her from it—least of all the man now standing in her room filling his pipe with short little loverlike movements. She was standing on a bridge that no longer touched the shore, and wherever she looked she saw only fog, darkness and water. Discovery was not a game any more. It was of no use even to be strong, or to creep into his arms and make a rampart of his flesh; because discovery was not a lightning-like discharge, raging for a moment and then over; discovery was a state of monotonous torment, an endless topic of conversation for a few hundred peasants, lumbermen and officials, and the womenfolk of all these. That was what frightened her so. The air was full of Fru Mattsson's eyes. That was what made her scream.

'I'm tired of it all,' she cried. 'I'm tired of having the whole village spying round the house. I'm tired of seeing people leer whenever I go outside the gate. I'm tired of seeing people huddling together and whispering as soon as they see my bicycle along the road. I'm tired of being the forester's whore.'

'Alice, has anyone said that?'

'And you—you're too stupid to see what's under your very nose. If you really minded about me you wouldn't expose me to all this. But you rate me about as high as a rotten apple. Oh, you—you——'

The forester put an arm round her head; the stuff of his sleeve was in her mouth, and when her words ceased to flow she was desperately tired and allowed him to lead her into his room. She lay on his bed, stroking the flowered counterpane with the palms of her hands. Outside it was raining, the windowpanes were blurred with water, and in the arbour the cakes would be getting rained to mush and there would be water in the cups and the cream jug, but she hadn't the strength to go down. She lay and listened to the forester, who was sitting at the writing table brandishing a penknife.

He was saying that of course he understood perfectly well —he knew what it was like when a potty little village like this began gossiping about a married woman having someone besides her husband; but really it was only the scarf business that had been stupid. He admitted it. That was something that *might* pass for some sort of evidence. But in other ways hadn't they always been careful? Had she ever been in his room when her husband came home from school? Had he so much as touched her when anyone else was there? Had they ever shown themselves together on the road or in the public gardens? And how careful they'd been about their meetings, telling the husband that the forester would be out in the woods all next day, while she cut sandwiches for him in the kitchen to allay misgivings. And hadn't he always set off early on those mornings, and lurked in the woods until he knew school had begun? And how cunningly he had come back, always by tracks and paths, always ready to dive into a thicket at the least sound.

'But don't forget that Arne came home today,' said the schoolmaster's wife quietly. 'We might easily have been in your room then.'

'Arne came home,' said the forester calmly. 'He had seen the scarf on the hat-shelf, wondered where it had come from and drawn his own conclusions. He must have been reassured to find us having coffee when he tried to take us by surprise.'

'And Fru Mattsson,' said the schoolmaster's wife. 'She had

127

never discovered before that it's a short cut to go through our garden, although she was born and bred here.'

'Fru Mattsson,' said the forester, carving a ruler with his knife. 'I expect Fru Mattsson met Arne in the woods and began wondering.'

'How could you be such a fool as to call me when you knew she was here!'

'I thought she'd gone, and anyhow there's nothing odd about my calling to you, after living here all this time.'

'But you swore, and people only swear at their mistresses.'

'I admit I've been careless,' said the forester placidly, trying to see out through the tear-blinded window. 'Perhaps we've both been careless. You needn't have worn the scarf when you went to the shop. But nothing's past curing—not even carelessness. You can cure that by being twice as careful as before. You and I will be so careful that everybody will be ashamed of suspecting us, and take it all back. If ever we've looked at each other when we've had coffee with Arne in the evenings we'll never give so much as a glance in future. Do you think you can guard your eyes?'

'If you can, I can,' said the schoolmaster's wife, and all at once she felt very tired. She looked at the rain streaming down the window. A butcher's shop-window, she thought, and laughed a little—just a tiny laugh, hardly noticeable. At any rate the forester noticed nothing. He opened the zip-fastener of his tobacco-pouch, took a pinch of tobacco and crumbled it on the floor.

'We'll be polite to each other, but no more. Definitely no more,' he went on.

'Definitely not,' said the schoolmaster's wife. 'Definitely not. Definitely not.'

The forester was surprised when she said it the third time.

Sometimes she used to tease him with her damned superiority, and repeat his words in her voice but with his tone. It was like looking at oneself in a cracked looking-glass. 'How long are you going to keep that up?' he would ask her, and she would reply, 'As long as I want to.' And she wanted to for a long time—so long that at last, maddened, he thrust her down on the bed and her lips became a magnet, drawing his to them.

The rain poured and poured. The forester had lit his pipe and was pulling in the smoke with childishly rounded lips. On the writing table ticked his alarm-clock, which usually rang at one in the afternoon, when the blind was drawn. 'Definitely not,' thought Alice, but didn't remember why. The forester took his pipe from his mouth.

'The whole trick is to wait,' he said, stroking his pipe-stem. 'Can you learn to wait?'

'What for?'

'For the right moment. Isn't Arne going on that school outing?'

'On June the sixth,' Alice said, sitting on the edge of the bed and looking out at the sky that was clearing over the garden—looking over the forester's head and straight into a cloud. He had to stand up to exceed this height. He walked up and down the room, stepping aside for her feet each time, but never touching her.

'In a fortnight,' he said, stopping by the window. 'Can you wait that long?'

She looked at his back as he said this. Tremble a little, she prayed; but the forester's back was quite still. She rose from the bed and walked over the silencing mat to the door—walked backwards to see whether the mute back would notice her; but the back was blind and noticed nothing.

But when her own back brushed against the door the

forester turned slowly and sitting on the windowsill he said, without a tremor in his voice,

'Well, then, for a fortnight we won't notice each other. Do you think you can manage that?'

But the schoolmaster's wife didn't say exactly what he expected. She curtsied there in front of the door, with grace and mockery; she curtsied and said,

'Until we meet again, *Herr* forester.'

When he was alone once more he sat down at the writing-table and looked through a book on hunting. He wound up his alarm-clock and set it for midnight. Presently he stole to the door and turned the key. In the drawer of the writing table he had a little bottle of French brandy, for use in times of stress, and taking the glass from the water-carafe he poured a little—a very little—into the bottom of it. He poured out exactly the amount that a man of character would pour. He held the glass up against the light, glad that he had taken so little. Then he tossed it back in a single, painful gulp. He poured himself out the same amount several times, and each time was just as pleased with his strength of character.

The sun came out very suddenly and hit him in the eyes. When he leaned forward over the writing table to pull down the blind against it, he saw Alice coming from the arbour carrying the remains of their interrupted meal on a red tray that cast a kindly glow on the grass as she walked. Her shoulders were tired and she seemed to be leaning on the tray, bearing her fatigue and her incipient despair upon it, and keeping her eyes rigidly fixed upon it so as to lose nothing. Then the forester was seized by a sudden tenderness for her, and as he bent across the writing-table with his eyes following her quiet progress towards the house he felt that pleasurable tenderness warming his body.

Dear little woman, he said with his mouth shut and his throat still, nevertheless feeling that his words passed out into the room and lay motionless on its thick air, smelling of kindness—the forester's kindness. He was filled with unspeakable relief, and as he did not want to be clear about the reason for this relief he told himself that it arose from his tactful handling of the business of Alice and the schoolmaster. When Alice had disappeared into the house he felt he deserved yet another gulp of brandy, and as a reward he poured out a shade more perhaps than befitted a man of character. Then he locked away the bottle and took his gun from the wardrobe. Laying it across the writing-table he flicked away with a piece of blotting-paper any dust that might have settled on the barrel. He removed the breech-piece and closed his eyes while he fingered its hard, gleaming surfaces. For a whole week the gun had been put away in the wardrobe, and he slipped the piece in again with smooth, tender movements. He raised the gun, put the butt to his shoulder and aimed at the arbour. There ought to have been an owl there, or a sparrow at least. Or some bottles. His pet notion for target-practice was to have bottles suspended from balloons and fire at them through the window from a chair, or even lying on his bed. There were no bottles, owls or sparrows, but the gate into the woods had squeaked. It was the schoolmaster returning, hot, carrying a bundle of exercise-books under his arm, and smoking. Too late the forester found himself aiming at him with his gun. Unloaded, certainly, but it was a stupid thing to have happened.

The schoolmaster found his wife in the kitchen. She was drying china—coffee-cups and plates which must very recently have been standing on a tray, for the tray was not hung up in its place but was still on the table, with marks of spilt coffee on it. All this he noted before greeting her, sitting down on a stool and detonating the bomb.

'You didn't come your usual way,' his wife remarked, as she wiped the tray and hung it on the wall.

'I came through the woods,' he said, weighing the exercise-books in one hand. 'I had the idea it was a bit shorter, but perhaps I was wrong.'

'Fru Mattsson came through there today. She thought it was shorter too.'

'I shan't do it again,' said the schoolmaster, and looked so intently at her that at last she couldn't keep her eyes steady.

'Oh, why not?' she asked uncertainly.

Bang!

The man had dropped the books on the table. He allowed a moment of silence to pass before continuing.

'I don't want to be shot dead through a window,' he said at last, so coolly that what he said was doubly shattering.

His wife sank down on a chair; they sat at opposite sides of the table looking deep into each other's eyes, and this time her gaze was steady. But it was from amazement, not fear and a guilty conscience as her husband imagined.

'Shot?' she repeated, smiling foolishly because it sounded so absurdly novelettish.

Her husband rose slowly, his eyes still plunged in hers like those of a lion-tamer.

'The forester was standing in his room aiming his gun at me,' he said, in as matter-of-fact a tone as before.

The woman's face turned fiery red and her eyes fell, fell uncontrollably. The man saw this, turned ostentatiously and walked over to the window. Helplessly the woman looked at his back. At first she wanted to jump up, spin him round and hurl at him every word she could think of in defence of the forester; but when her flush had subsided she grew calm, and as at last she pushed her chair back she found a way of saving the dignity, conscience and feelings of them all.

'Arne,' she said, and repeated the name insistantly until he turned to her. 'Arne, you must go up to him at once and ask for an explanation. If not for your own sake then for mine. Do you think I'd dare be alone in the house with a lunatic who aims guns at people? I shan't have a moment's peace. Besides, it's a punishable offence. Tell him that.'

Together they went upstairs, and it was Alice who led the way, though without touching Arne. She walked ahead. Her husband followed her unwillingly, half-stunned by a strange and gladdening fact—or two facts. 'Lunatic' she had said— she had called the forester a lunatic, and in that sharp tone. And 'punishable'. 'Besides, it's a punishable offence.' And so he followed her.

The forester stood in the doorway, broadshouldered and tousled. He blinked at them stupidly as if he'd been asleep and had been suddenly roused. Alice was quick and wouldn't wait for him to get his breath.

'My husband tells me you pointed your gun at him as he came through the garden just now,' she said.

The forester stepped backwards into the room, sat down on the edge of the writing-table and fingered his knees. He stammered a little, shamefacedly.

'A mistake,' he said, looking at the floor. 'I wanted to see if the gun was clean, and so I put it to my shoulder. It was just too bad that Arne happened to be there, but——'

'Yes, I see,' said Arne. 'It shook me for a moment, that's all. I just happened to look up and see it.'

On the stairs he asked his wife suddenly, in a low voice close to her ear,

'Since when have you stopped saying "thou" to him?' Alice halted and looked up into his face with desperate resolution.

'Today. He said something silly about your coming home in the middle of the day. I told him I wouldn't have that kind of talk. He'd given me a scarf, too. I expect you've seen it?'

'No,' he lied, concerned to hide his jealousy for the sake of following the scent.

She took it down from the shelf while he studied her smile, comparing it with others on similar occasions to decide whether it was false. She watched his face as he looked at the scarf, and saw by the exaggerated care with which he examined it that he had known about it already. This made her a little uneasy; she stepped out of herself and stood by, correcting every gesture before she made it, that all might carry conviction.

The forester didn't come down for coffee that evening. They heard him pacing up and down his room for a time. Then he lay down on the bed; the springs creaked, and after that it was long before any sound was heard from upstairs.

'He's sulky, of course,' Alice said when her husband commented on his absence. 'Sulky first because I snubbed him earlier on, and then because of that gun business.'

It was plausible. As the schoolmaster spread honey on a wheaten roll he scrutinised different parts of his wife's face, but all looked genuine. Later that night, when they had just got into bed, they heard the forester's heavy tread on the stairs. He went straight out and away towards the woods. The schoolmaster lay on his back in bed, cool and clear-headed, weighing things up, judging. On the one hand he set the incriminating documents and on the other the ones testifying to innocence. His wife crept over into his bed; he was glad of

134

this at first, and then suspicious, as it was nearly always he who took the initiative. He lay mute beside her, the items of guilt and innocence in his mind, but the warmer he grew from her the more immersed he became in the evidence of her innocence. At last he felt freer and happier than for a long time, and fell asleep late with her hair between his teeth.

She lay awake for some time after he had fallen asleep, and parts of the day repeated themselves before her mind's eye. Cautiously she freed herself from him, and when coolness came she could have cried out with pain over the fortnight that separated her from happiness—that sweet, fierce happiness—the happiness that bites. She did not cry out, but lay long awake.

At dawn the forester came home. Alice was woken by the noise on the verandah. The room was very warm and she rose to open a window. A heavy thud came from the verandah, and immediately afterwards hard footsteps crashed on the stairs. She remembered then that he had been out that night, but all the same she went barefoot on to the verandah to see what had caused the thud. A great white bundle lay tossed on the floor and she stopped short in horror at the sight of a stiff white wing with blood at its edges—a frozen wave of blood and feathers. The shot bird, the raw mists creeping through the garden, and the menacing silence that lay over the village flung her back into the house and over to the looking-glass. She stood in front of the glass, rubbing the blood back into her cheeks and feeling very sorry for herself standing there, scared and alone.

I must speak to him, she thought, now at once. He's got to help me—he can't leave me alone. She took the scarf from the shelf and wound it about her head. Having listened outside the bedroom and heard no sound she ran lightly up the stairs, hardly daring to touch the treads for fear of discovery. She didn't knock at the forester's door: a knock might have woken one who had to go on sleeping. Instead she opened it very softly.

She opened it so softly that she took him by surprise. Suddenly she was standing on the threshold of his room, conscious of feeling cold. She would have liked to turn and race downstairs because what she saw filled her with such repugnance that at first she thought she could not endure it without screaming. There are some situations in which we do not care to see those we love, because the unworthiness of their behaviour wounds our pride. Their meanness becomes in all respects our own, and only by breaking with them abruptly can we save our dignity.

There was a long moment of silence by the door, but the forester had seen nothing. Slowly her eyes filled with hot tears. Insulted and forsaken she stood there, imprinting on her mind every detail of the scene before her. She looked at the glass in the man's right hand. Nearly full, she thought. What a sensualist! When he doesn't want me he turns to brandy. She saw him in profile—that drunken, bloated, red, contented profile. How could she have loved it? Or had she never seen it before? And that left hand; her gaze lingered there particularly, because it was the way in which that hand was occupied that fascinated and filled her with disgust.

The forester had shot a squirrel, a big, handsome animal, and it was lying across his knees. He was stroking it with his left hand, not gently, but like a delighted possessor. He didn't look cruel, merely satisfied. As satisfied as when women give themselves to him, she thought. The type who can love only with his hands.

Naturally he was bound to see her in the end; one cannot

think so intently about a person without his sensing it. A sharp thought had scratched his cheek. He turned sluggishly, the caressing hand clenched in defence. As soon as he saw her he tried to get up, to bring his dignity to its feet, but she signed to him to keep still. To be found sitting! If he had been standing he would at least have been able to look down at her; he felt himself shrinking until his shoulders were little more than a hanger for his shooting jacket.

'What are you doing here?' he asked sombrely, removing the glass as surreptitiously as he could.

'You don't usually ask me that,' the schoolmaster's wife replied, feeling the rough wood of the threshold beneath her feet. It hurt her, but braced her. Let things hurt, so long as they reminded her of her duty to her hatred. Carefully she loosened the forester's coloured scarf from about her hair.

The forester let her do it. He did not spring up and besiege her with pleas to keep it on, or ask her how she could be so cruel as to reject a present which he had given her with all his heart. No, he sat still, choosing his words. He stayed in his chair instead of leaping up and taking her by storm, although he told himself that this might be a solution. He sat still because she had caught him out and, what was worse, he felt caught out. And to feel caught out is to find oneself in the dock, even though no accusations are made. So he sat in his chair, preparing his defence; and what more effective defence than to cut from under the accuser's feet the moral grounds on which he has taken his stand?

The forester turned slowly and looked at his glass. There wasn't much in it; hardly anything; it was almost as empty as the glass of a man of character should be. So he raised it from the writing-pad and holding it in his hand as an argument for his own excellence he swung round upon her. There was an ominous gleam in his eyes. Me! he thought—with exclamation-mark—can't I even sit in the room I pay rent for and enjoy a little drop of brandy in my solitude? And the game I shoot—mayn't I take it up to my expensive room without her making a scandal of it? And is it for her to talk like that, he thought (although she hadn't said a word). Her! She's so sunk in hypocrisy that she forces other people to practise it too—forces them to say they never touch a drop or that it would never occur to them to shoot animals for pleasure. She's tried to demoralise me, that's what she's done, but she shan't gain a thing by it. Now it was he who was doing the catching out. As if he didn't know just why she was forcing herself on him at this hour. So he took a little gulp to clear his throat and then said,

'Didn't we agree not to meet like this for another fortnight?'

His voice was thick with suppressed emotion. This sudden attempt upon his excellence brought tears to his eyes—or at least dimmed them. Steam from the fury boiling within him condensed on the windows of his soul.

It came at last, the Scene—the Big Scene—the one that a man would hide his eyes from if he were less polite. The bare white feet of the schoolmaster's wife had left the threshold of torment and were standing on the soft carpet, quivering with the desire to kick and the longing to run away. Unexpectedly she didn't scream: her voice was a tightrope on which her words balanced their way forward; if one word were too heavy the rope would snap.

'You have a lovely time, don't you!' she said. 'You with your gun and your brandy. You don't need to lie awake at night, yearning. Nobody gossips about you in shops and farm-kitchens. Nobody thinks you're ridiculous. Nobody thinks you're shameful, because you're not deceiving anybody

—nobody but me. But what about me! Everybody loves to see a deceiver deceived. For you a fortnight passes easily— it's just a nice little holiday. Imagine—two whole weeks without having to be kissed! How lovely! Fancy not having to be in love for a fortnight. What a wonderful time some people do have.'

But the forester appeared quite unmoved. And indeed he was, for the simple reason that he didn't understand what she was saying. He was merely waiting for her to stop so that he could come out with his Line—the one that would procure him final peace and declare plainly on whose side Justice lay. Not even a playwright who, in the middle of a blazing dress rehearsal, suddenly hits on the Line Irresistible, could have awaited with greater eagerness an opportunity to make his voice heard. And suddenly the schoolmaster's wife fell silent. Her feet were no longer trembling; they were rooted fast in the forester's rug and would not move until she had heard the plea for forgiveness from his lips. Not that she wanted to forgive—but who dislikes playing god to a person's prayers? The forester sat up in his chair till it creaked, and straightened his back, with steady eyes and a rigid face. His hand hardened round the glass. Lucky it's not celluloid, she thought. With celluloid you'd be lost.

'I am a man of character,' said the forester. He stressed the 'I' and assumed a look of dignified grief as he said it, as if infinitely pained at having to remind his listener of so evident a fact. He emptied his glass. Not even brandy disordered the face controlled by such stern sentiments.

But for the schoolmaster's wife this meant the end. As she stood there she was suddenly staring down into Fru Mattsson's face. Fru Mattsson's eyes gazed inexorably into hers, in judgment. 'You have no character,' those eyes said. 'You're lost, abandoned, shamed in this village.' She wanted to scream, but a person who is alone—alone in the absolute sense of the word—does not scream out her despair; it is useless. Deserts do not hear. But she can do things with her hands which even a desert must notice. She can tear at the sand until the desert bleeds.

Tsss!—and two halves of a coloured scarf lay on the forester's massive knees. The woman no longer stood rooted before him. With a bitten off sob she fled, wildly, uncontrolably, and thus strengthened the forester's belief in the justice of his cause. The man who can control himself always fancies himself in the right. The door slammed. 'Hysterical fool,' he thought dispassionately, and sank back into his non-dignified attitude. 'She has shut that door for the last time. Must have a drop more brandy,' and he re-filled his glass. Presently he took his gun and aimed carefully into the air. But no brandy-bottle came sailing in a balloon out of the thin, cold mists of dawn.

The schoolmaster had been dreaming of voices. The slam of a door woke him and made him sit up in bed. Then, as his wife opened the doors on her way in to him he lay down again in the agonising conviction that he knew all. The remembered pleasures of the early part of the night still lingered in his limbs as he wrapped the bedclothes round him. It was humiliating to have made love so recently with someone who was unfaithful. It made a man accessory to the crime but did nothing to stiffen his indignation. Nothing is so paralysing to the will as the memory of shared delight. The schoolmaster resolved to feign sleep when his wife came in.

She resolved to wake him. The warmth with which she tried to caress him into wakefulness soon convinced him that something must have happened between her and the forester;

perhaps indeed everything was over between them. But the thought brought him no comfort. The fact itself, the most humiliating of all, remained: while he slept she had released herself from his arms and gone up to another man's room. And who could tell whether she had done this to provoke a scene? Betrayal in one's own absence may possbily be forgiven; it is like betraying one's soul. But that one's warm body should be betrayed was beyond forgiveness. The schoolmaster made his body stiff, but at last he was compelled to respond so as not to reveal his deception. He performed a prolonged, elaborate stage-awakening, stretching himself in all directions, blinking as realistically as possible, yawning and producing a few unintelligible words from his throat. His wife slipped her hand inside his pyjama-jacket. Before he was properly awake, and with his eyes still shut, he took his wife's wrist and removed her hot hand from his skin. He wanted to demonstrate to her how sternly his subconscious condemned the betrayal. As soon as his eyes were open and natural she said, moving in from the edge of the bed towards him.

'Arne, take me with you.'

'Where to?' asked the schoolmaster, in a far more wide-awake voice than he intended.

But she was so desperately afraid of being forsaken once more, so afraid of the desert, that she noticed nothing improbable in her husband's behaviour.

'On the school outing,' she almost sobbed, trying to catch his eyes, catch eyes that loved her, looked at her as they had looked three hours before: black and shining with desire.

Her husband sat up in bed and stared out at the garden. The memories of his desire had slackened their hold and his body became as heavy and staid as if it were pregnant. The school outing, he thought, while little scenes from school, superficially innocent but in their context terrible, besieged his mind's eye. Little girls' heads close together, their eyes sliding rapidly, ashamedly, over his person. A girl shouting 'the forester!' in a corridor, two masters falling suddenly silent when he walked unexpectedly into the common room. A whole busload of clustering heads, with eyes stealthily observing them both for three hundred and fifty miles. No thank you.

'Out of the question,' he said curtly. He could afford to be wide awake now.

'But why not?' she pleaded, believing to the last that there was some technical reason to prevent it.

Her husband settled himself comfortably back in bed. He braced his narrow shoulders as for a gymnastic display, then clasped his hands over his stomach: a man pregnant with his dignity.

'I am a man of character,' he said. ('I'm ashamed' sounded egoistic. 'I'm afraid' sounded cowardly. But 'I'm a man of character' was just right.)

But no sooner had the words been uttered than his wife was transformed before his eyes—those eyes that were so full of character—into a little bundle quivering in paroxysms of laughter, rolling about on the bed. So hardened, he thought, that she can't even cry.

A weeping woman is very convenient. One can comfort and forgive a weeping woman without loss of face. It can even give a man pleasure to inject his solace into a woman who weeps. But laughter! Laughing despair is just not permissible; there is nothing to be done with a woman who laughs. Nothing but let her laugh. And draw the bedclothes over one's head, turn on one's side and go back to sleep.

NOCTURNAL
RESORT

Nocturnal Resort

ONE may well wonder why bathing resorts are dirtier than almost any other sort of place. It may be that too much bathing goes on there—too much washing—so that all the dirt that people usually carry with them is rubbed off and left lying about; in the little reedy inlets, for instance, in the carefully fenced back gardens, and along the by-ways that wind so capriciously through the woods along the coast. Beaches which we would least suspect of such a thing turn out, when we let the dinghy drift ashore, to be lined with a regular barrier of eggshells and old newspapers, and brown bottles that knock against the stones with the sound of a station telegraph. Having with the greatest repugnance dragged the boat ashore through this unappetising fringe, we find ourselves in a dump of old food tins, carelessly opened, twisted, grinning at the visitor with ends that are still shiny, while in the bushes sadly discoloured newspapers feebly flap their drowned world history. We seem to be visiting a museum of the day before yesterday—that eerily dead day, deader than anything else: deader than last year or the year before, deader than 1936 or 1928 or 1912, because from those more faraway times museum grime has been washed away and consumed by many clean winds and strong rains.

We wander, oppressed, among these memories, and in the end it becomes too much for us: we start to imagine a lot of foolishness: we hear the tins repeating snatches of human dialogue and bursts of laughter first uttered at the meals they had the pleasure of attending during their brief existence. Here at least we might have hoped to find some variety, but the fragments of conversation we pick up are so nightmarishly alike that at last, revolted, we stick our fingers in our ears. It's like listening to an SOS on the wireless and then, on opening the window, seeing a whole queue of people waiting outside the dairy, all answering to the wanted person's description.

We run to the tattered newspapers in the hope of hearing a little sense from them, at least; and at first, to our relief, we do detect the clash of contradiction, and bursts of excitement alternating with idle statement. Yet if we listen long enough —and this depends upon whether we can stand the smell— we soon find that these exchanges were nothing but illusion; that the heat and passion generated perhaps in the former possessors of these papers were just as meaningless as laziness and indifference: a parlour-game, the briefest of pastimes.

At last, enraged, we shove the boat out again, slipping on the eggshells and cursing them, and head straight for the open sea and its blue rim, which is crinkled now and then like a fishing-line by the waves. But before long the red life-boat glides away from the jetty and races after us—and in the end we lie down in the bilge and let ourselves drift into the very jaws of the red parasols and grotesque rubber animals on the beach, while every sounding-board within us reverberates its protest: the day before yesterday, that damned day before yesterday! Is that all there was to be had out of it? A few foolishly chattering newspapers and tins? Is that all that survives of the present, after forty-eight hours have passed? Cursed be this museum of our dead days and our dead lives, and cursed be the slackness and criminal irresponsibility of the local authorities, who allow visitors to compromise themselves and each other at will!

2

Sisyphos, who bears his doomed name with heroic equanimity, is glad to take you over the abandoned lighthouse which stands up like a lone marrow-bone from among the pleasant green of the landscape, and to show you the bathing-resort from above. Any equipment that would remind one of the building's former purpose has been removed and taken to other lighthouses. This tower is chemically clean of life, with its whitewashed walls where not even a fly seems able to find foothold; the winding stairs are as slippery as slides, and the air reluctantly entering through the slits of windows seems purer than the usual kind. Yes, the lighthouse tower is certainly the cleanest place in the whole resort—and this is entirely owing to Sisyphos. He is the only one with a key to the wind-worn door; his uncle was the last of the lighthouse-keepers here, and not everyone is allowed in. They say he wanders about the beach, seemingly as absent-minded and casual as the dun-coloured dogs of the place, but in fact searching with sombre energy for faces that appeal to him; faces belonging to people who probably won't mess up the stairs, and drop silver paper on every other step and orange-peel on every third, stub out cigarettes against the white walls and try to spit on the chapel when at last they reach the little platform at the top, where the sea, a flock of islands, a lean, stony strip of coast and the blue-green woods inland lie spread defencelessly beneath them.

Sisyphos believes in facial expression as an index of character, but he sometimes makes mistakes. Once, for instance, a party of visitors with a jovial look about them dropped a whole battery of bottles down the stairs, just to see whether they would arrive intact at the bottom. Only some of them did, and the tower was filled with broken glass and dirty puddles of some evil-smelling liquid. But usually, of course, he is right, and once he has taken a fancy to your face he won't leave you, and follows you everywhere with relentless perseverence. If you hire a boat, you may be sure that Sisyphos will get hold of one too, and stay obstinately near you, however rough the sea may be; at a restaurant he will always sit at the next table and observe you unflinchingly, even while drinking; it is both comic and embarrassing to see his fixed, staring eyes above the rim of the glass. And when at last he follows you into your rented garden and paces resolutely back and forth among the croquet-hoops, you give up and ask him dryly what he wants.

Then he stops, scratches the back of his neck reflectively and says in a reluctant tone, 'Yes, well—I suppose you want to see the lighthouse.' He sounds as if he were against the idea, but suddenly, lightly, he catches you by the sleeve, draws you out of the garden and up the steep mound, into the tower and up the unending stairs, which suck the strength from your very bones.

But once up there, you feel that no price could be too high for the experience; you forget to mop your forehead and hang over the rail in sheer rapture, letting the sweat drip. You can find no words for your delight; from two hundred and thirty feet up the dirty bathing-resort is a thing of beauty; the roofs lie at anchor in the verdure; the yellow paths wind like lost hair-ribbons and seem to be lightly, so lightly, exhaling their dust.

Then, while still transfixed by this loveliness, you become conscious of Sisyphos' presence. He clears his throat vigorously and purposefully as one desiring to prepare the world for a long and important speech; then he grasps your arm so violently that you cling to the rail in alarm, lest you fall. His mighty aquiline nose has whitened at the nostrils and his mouth seems on the point of emitting blood and gall.

'Do you see her?' he almost shrieks. 'Do you see her down there, the old trollop? She's crawled in among the bushes with her lover, thinking nobody can see her shamelessness. But oh, how wrong she is! It makes everything worse when people try to hide and don't know how. Watch her closely now; she hasn't even the sense to grow old decently, like other tarts—she thinks this kind of thing can go on for ever —and it's long, long ago since she crossed the boundary line.'

He lets go of your arm and stands just behind you, breathing down your neck. And behold—at once the view is disfigured; notwithstanding the great height you can see that the roofs are rotting and that their owners have tried to hide this by slapping on masses of paint, a few brittle tiles, and shiny bits of sheet iron, rendering the whole effect yet more pitiful, like that of a raddled old prostitute—yes, that is an apt comparison. The fine paths are littered with smashed petrol cans which look like trampled beetles, and round the islands and rocks out at sea the rims of refuse bob up and down like big dead worms, while an ugly, ungainly steamer drags horrible banks of yellow smoke after her as she waddles across the bay.

'How disgusting,' you say, 'how vile. What has become of all the loveliness? Why did you have to say that? It was so beautiful before.'

You have come down again, and are standing in the scent of jasmine by the tower, trying to wash your eyes in the lush greenery—but all in vain.

'Yes, well,' says Sisyphos modestly as he locks the door, 'it's my job, that's all. Just my job.'

He tests the lock once or twice to make sure that no unauthorised person can break in and rob the tower of its solitude.

'Your job?'

149

But Sisyphos doesn't answer; he's already on his way up the jasmine slope with a long, determined stride. Suddenly he dives through a gap in a hedge, having no doubt caught sight of some new tower-climber ruminating among the croquet-hoops. The air, the road, the whole place is full of the smell of jasmine—and all one wants to do is to spit it out, spit until one is free of it. If one only could! If it was just a matter of spitting!

3

The things that are done for money, the deeds the veriest coward will perform for a reasonable reward! Here, as in many other places, half-grown boys dive from quite a high cliff for coins dropped into the sea by visitors. The hotel staff bring chairs out on to this cliff for those who would rather be up here than throw their money from the little quay below. But those who prefer the quay seem to find it very exciting to watch how near the edge of it the boys dive. Once indeed a boy cracked his skull when going after a two-crown piece dropped just over the brink. Nowadays as a rule the coins are not so big, for it was found that the lads were just as willing to dive for twenty-five öre bits; and one of the lovelies from the hotel walks about smilingly with a bag of small coins on her stomach, changing the visitors' notes.

Early in the morning the boys gather outside the hotel, making a deliberate noise to induce the guests to swallow their ham and eggs with all speed and hurry off to the chairs on the diving-cliff. Many of the more elderly ladies and gentlemen, who are the ones who most often indulge in this amusement, follow the graceful arched flight of those brown bodies with secret desire:. they fancy they are watching a flock of nature-children sporting innocently with death; for it must never leak out that the boys are engaged by the hotel to provide this extra entertainment. For the most part these boys come from very poor families in the villages along the coast, and from eight o'clock to six every day their mothers go in constant terror of a faulty dive, too short a spring, a head striking the edge of the quay, or an irresponsible visitor, who might tempt them to take greater risks than usual. But their fathers, whose chief occupation is fishing among the banks of refuse left by tourist steamers—and the most astonishing things can be found there!—take the matter more calmly. What will happen will happen, they say, spitting out into the seaweed as they watch out for more dirt-shedding vessels, and so it has always been.

But of course accidents do happen. There would be even more of them if it weren't for all the good luck there is in the world, and at this resort in particular. Here, for instance, one of the boys loves a rich young married woman called Pepita. What the boy's name is we don't know; it's the kind of thing one never does know. The woman, whose husband is a successful stockbroker and who has rings instead of children, sat in a comfortable chair at the very edge of the cliff. With nervous grace she dropped streams of silver coins into the water, which is so clear that one can follow the movements of the boys' bodies against the sea-bed like those of goldfish in an aquarium. The boy who loves her—only she doesn't know it, being too lazy and arrogant to observe anyone but herself—always dived from her place: a risky habit, as a sharp point of rock juts out just beneath. But the boy was encouraged by her throwing in so much money, not understanding that people can squander from sheer indifference. Nor, luckily, did he know anything of her abstracted yawns when in his eagerness to please he performed artistic deep dives, right down to the bed of shells.

151

But one day the inevitable happened: the young woman, whose fingers were so stiff with rings that one couldn't touch her hand without getting scratched, tossed a valuable ring into the water by mistake. She noticed it just as it struck the surface of the sea, and uttered a short, shrill scream. But her admirer was already on his way down; he met the water with his body tense and beautiful with longing; the long, delicate hands that split the surface seemed almost to detach themselves from the wrists in their desire to grasp the sinking ring; and down there in the silent green world he could be seen swiftly and gracefully plunging to the faintly gleaming floor. When he came up again his young face was quivering with triumph, and he shook the water from his hair with a movement of uncontrolled joy. He must have been thinking: 'Oh, at last—at last a reward for my steadfast, silent love.' With the ring on his little finger he sat for a time on the edge of the quay under the diving-rock, trying to digest his happiness.

Then Pepita discovered that the ring she had lost was in fact the most valuable of all; when the boy didn't bring it back she grew anxious and screamed without restraint.

'Come along, now! How much longer must I wait? Bring that ring back, can't you?'

The girl who changed money was very tender of the reputation of the hotel and of the whole resort; she grasped the boy's arm and led him up to the worried young woman; and as he slowly drew off the ring he must have grasped, for all his inexperience, the full extent of Pepita's egoism, coldness and lovelessness. For with an abrupt movement he threw himself backwards over the edge of the cliff—and when he was dragged out the back of his head and neck had been slit open by a sharp point of rock. Some of the boys carried him up towards the back steps of the hotel, while blood

dripped all over the top of the cliff. Most of the visitors like
to think that he'll live, and the cynical old retired colonel
soothed everybody's conscience by saying,

'Lucky. Might have been a lot worse.' And he changed a
whole fifty-crown note with the ever-smiling girl.

Pepita remained sitting on the cliff-top, obstinately en-
grossed in her rings, and whenever anyone approached she
burst out hysterically,

'What a little twister, trying to get away with it like that!
Well, as usual, I'll be lenient—mercy before justice. As
usual!'

The colonel too became involved in quite a nasty business
of the same kind. His favourite diver, a frail but active boy
with brown, girlish curls, had weak lungs; and after every
dive he would double up and cough. One morning his mother,
a poor woman, came on to the cliff top and shouted before
anyone could stop her,

'This can't go on any longer, d'you hear? There must be
no more of it. This morning he could hardly get out of bed
after coughing all night. It's his lungs, you see.'

Just then everybody heard the boy coughing down on the
beach, hollowly and with a rattle, like a burst drum.

'There you are!' cried the mother triumphantly. 'What did
I tell you? You can hear what he's like.'

But afterwards, when she had taken him by the arm and
the two of them were on their way down towards the rowing-
boat in which she had arrived, the colonel shouted after them
in the sort of voice which announces that its owner can afford
to shout what he likes,

'Come back, boy! You don't want to lose a whole day's
wage for just a bit of a chill. One more little dive, and you'll
be better in no time.'

Red with defiance and shyness the boy tore himself away from his mother and rushed up on to the cliff. The colonel had already thrown the big coin and it was sinking rapidly to the bottom. To catch it before it disappeared in the sand the boy made a quick, powerful spring, and they saw him plunge vertically through the water without so much as a quiver of his body. But then a twitch ran through his right leg, like the last, pitiful tail-flap of a dying fish; in a horizontal position the body sank down to the bottom, pressed against the sand and lay motionless, like a drowned submarine. They dived for him but he was already dead, and all the onlookers went away, to spare the mother's feelings and their own nerves.

Only the colonel took the accident heroically. Next morning he was back as usual on the rock, and a thin, cheeky little boy was doing his utmost to please him. Gradually all the rest of the party turned up, and out of consideration for the colonel's feelings they all tactfully avoided mentioning yesterday's incident. Everything went on as usual; coins flashed in the sun, and with shining bodies and dripping hair the boys clambered out of the water and stacked up their catch on the stones of the beach.

But in the heat of noon a small rowing-boat headed slowly in towards the rock; while it was still some way out the occupant shipped the streaming oars and let the craft drift ashore. Soon everyone could see that it was the dead boy's mother, and there was a general feeling that it was abominably tactless of her to appear like this so soon after the tragedy. She sprang up suddenly so that the boat rocked, and screamed up at the cliff,

'Colonel Fels! Colonel Fels! I've got something for you.'

The colonel said nothing for a time, but his face grew hard and sharp-edged in his dread of defeat.

'What is it?' he growled at last.

'Colonel,' cried the woman, so agitated that the boat rocked as if it were in a heavy sea. 'Colonel, in this bag are my son's lungs. They're yours—you bought them, didn't you?'

With a couple of powerful strokes she reached the shore, but the money-changing girl was there before her, and prevented her from landing by kicking the boat out again.

'Make your complaints to the management!' she squealed in shrill falsetto. 'Complain to the management. Off you go to the management.'

The poor girl was quite red in the face.

4

As regards the sewer, there are those who say that it contains the most significant truth about a community, and that it merits respect rather than disdain. The main drain of the resort emerges discreetly behind a bush-clad point, and only when the wind is in the south can a faint, acrid odour be detected on the bathing-beach. It is fortunate for another reason too that the wind is so rarely in the south: the great rubber creatures that people love clinging to cannot then be towed out into deep water, for the seas run high. The creatures are of many different kinds: there are crocodiles, scarlet swans, sea-serpents, small whales and one or two fancy dolphins. It is touching to hear the more corpulent ladies, who have left even their second childhood behind them, crying as they waded through the thick water with a clumsy rubber swan pressed to their stomachs,

'I love swans—oh, how I love swans!'

The resort has other diversions to offer. There is one little group that lies under a large red parasol talking for days on end about Life, drinking unceasingly from tall, green glasses, and sweating. The leading spirit is a sinewy little man with grizzled hair and an arrogant profile, who claims to be a student of Life, though no one has ever seen him suffer. They seem to be vastly entertained by the kind of life that is lived here at the seaside and in many other places, and they sneer at everyone and everything: at football players, because no unsuccessful efforts look as unsuccessful as theirs; at croquet-players because their way of life demands that the earth should be as flat as a pancake; at bathers, because they pursue their pleasures in a constant state of fear: fear of jelly-fish, of cramp, bacteria and drowned persons. But if one asked Sisyphos about the group's qualifications, one felt less impressed.

'Oh, those——' he said, with a shrug as contemptuous as the heat allowed. 'Yes, they've been up the tower, but some of them were so much overcome by the view that they started to cry. They just stood there with their hands over their eyes, shaking and shaking; and when I said what I always say, and it was time to go down, one of them came up to me and said, 'Thank you for showing us; too bad about the prostitution —but all that will improve when they expand the police-force. But how beautiful it is—how marvellously beautiful!'

5

Can there be forgiveness for us—and if so, of what nature? And if there really were to be forgiveness, how are we to discover the form it would take, when we can't even agree upon the direction from which we're to expect it? Probably not even Sisyphos has thought the thing out properly, although he has wandered and pondered ever since he took over the lighthouse from his uncle. When he stands up there on the tower uttering his famous words, he means of course simply this: 'What we have done here is unpardonable—this beastliness, this sullying of a landscape to which roedeer, snakes and elk have an equal right—this pollution of water to which the smallest shrimp has a better right than we, since water is its element and not ours—and the irresponsible juggling with human life down on that cliff; the brutality we shut our eyes to because of the mixture of cowardice and sloth that fills our natures. If there is any pardon for these things, let us have it as soon as possible.'

When you have got on even better terms with Sisyphos he may perhaps, with a mysterious wink, ask you to come down to the big landing-stage at dusk, at that delightful hour when croquet-mallets no longer click and when the last gramophone has relapsed into silence—and no animal at the point of death can sound more despairing than a gramophone exhaling the last sigh of the day—when all the bawling people are sleeping it off and all the painfully loud lovers are slumbering in each others' arms, and for the first time since morning the birds are alone with their voices—then Sisyphos rows you straight out to sea.

At first you sit on the thwart quite scared, feeling the unfamiliar suck of the swell twisting under the boat, and expecting every moment to hear the life-boat splashing in pursuit of the rash fugitive; then you grow accustomed to the solitude of the hour, and when you turn and look towards the town you're already so far out that it looks like a little blue stone lying on a wide, deserted beach. All the repulsive house-profiles are swallowed up in darkness; the big, dirty hoardings are invisible too, and the water is blue with solitude; the vulgar rubber animals have vanished and the diving-cliff with its sombre memories has melted into the land. There is a pure, fresh smell in the long wind from the sea.

Suddenly the boat bumps gently against an islet, and boys who have lain hidden in the bushes rush up shouting and drag it far up the beach. Sisyphos is evidently expected; they greet him with perky respect, refreshingly different from the social tone of the resort. But soon they vanish again; we can hear them pushing out a raft, and amid cheerful splashing they tow it some way from the island. Then evidently they let it drift down the bay; all that can be heard is a soft, gay murmur from a floating point on the dark water, and then that too falls silent. These are the diving boys who spend their nights here, far beyond the stifling embrace of the seaside town.

'I've got my work, of course,' says Sisyphos, as we each sit on a stone and let our gaze patrol the coast. 'I've got my job; I show the view from the lighthouse as often as I can, but sometimes one has to rest one's eyes from the dirt, give them a cleansing bath—and only the nights are left for that. The only excuse—the only thing that gives the place a right to exist—is the night, these wonderful blue nights. Isn't it beautiful?'

'What was it like before?' we ask, for only now have we seen the tower holding up its wind-testing or perhaps monitory finger. 'What was it like in the days of the lighthouse?'

'Oh, about the same. There was a resort here then, too. Just about as dirty, but maybe the dirt was different—more natural, so to speak. There wasn't so much paper about, or so much tin and glass to cut oneself on, and I fancy they didn't look for excitement in such a brutal sort of way. But otherwise it was more or less the same.'

We smoke for a time in the darkness and hear the boys swimming back with the raft; then a sudden flare of light rises from the sea about three miles off, along the northern coast. It is a tall flame out on the sea, increasing in length and height, to stand at last like a wall of fire half a mile long, casting restlessly shifting shadows all the way to where we are sitting. For a moment the boys are brightly lit, and to our joy we see that their faces can breathe again, and are less convulsively bitter than in the daytime.

'It's the refuse-fishers setting fire to a bank of garbage,' says Sisyphos. 'There's often oil and carbide and other inflammable stuff in those drifts, and when the poor devils feel like letting off fireworks they set it alight, although they know they may be burning up a week's living. They live with open eyes; they don't shut them to dirt or beauty.'

Suddenly the wall of fire drops straight into the sea like a lowered net, and the dark is blinding. We sit quietly on our stones, hearing the boys' gay movements in the water, feeling the pulse-beat of the sea and listening to the soft rustling of newspapers in the bushes and the cheerful clinking of bottles at the edge of the water, and the merry clatter as the wind rinses out the empty food-tins. And from the little blue stone of a village on the shore we seem to hear a strange, beautiful murmur, like that of a sea-shell—and suddenly all of us out there in the darkness and solitude feel how we love the place —how painfully we love it. How painfully we long to be back in our nocturnal resort.

THE
SURPRISE

The Surprise

SOME people do nothing to be loved and yet are; others do everything, and are not. Really poor people, we may find, often find it difficult to be loved. When Åke's mother had been a widow for five years his grandfather celebrated his seventieth birthday. They were invited in a curt, eight-line letter, which said, 'Come if you like, but bring your own bedclothes because it's cold in the bedroom and some of you will have to sleep in the hall anyhow because there's more than you coming, we've asked the bank-manager and Jonsson the shopkeeper and they will have to sleep in the sitting-room and Elsa if you can come the day before to help with the cleaning and tables and cooking it would be a help. Yours, Irma. Afterwards we can manage the washing-up and that somehow and Åke can chop a bit of firewood.'

Åke's mother read the letter aloud one evening under the lamp. She was tired, and held on to the table with both hands. She had been washing ceilings all day long in a big flat in Östermalm, and had a headache from looking up at the sky for so long. When she had read the letter they both sat silent without looking at each other. Åke turned the pages of his geography book: 'The Trollhättan waterfalls are beautiful.' 'The Dutch are a cleanly nation: they scrub their pavements every day.' 'Under Mussolini's harsh but effective administration these unhealthy marshes have however been drained.' 'From Chile a fertilising substance called guano is exported.'

Åke's mother stared straight out into the room; her hands were utterly alone and they crumpled the letter into an uneven ball. When Åke looked at those hands they were ashamed, and smoothed the letter out, but it stayed as wrinkled as an old woman's face. The hands of the poor are always ashamed of what they're doing. That night the lamp on the writing table burned late, and it was a long time before Åke fell asleep. For a while he thought that his mother must have gone to sleep with the light on, but when he raised himself cautiously on his elbow and looked, he saw that her eyes were open and that the hands lying outside the bedclothes were crumpling and smoothing out an invisible letter.

Next night the lamp burned even longer. His mother sat fully dressed at father's old writing-table, and wrote. It was a letter that never seemed to get finished. Before Åke fell asleep the table was covered with crumpled, inky sheets of paper. In the middle of the night he woke up. It was cold, and his mother was sitting on his bed with her hand on his forehead, just as if he had a temperature. When he was quite awake she looked into his eyes and said,

'It's only twelve o'clock. How do you spell century—with a C or an S?'

The alarm-clock pointed to a quarter past one. 'C', he whispered. He heard her pad back to the table and begin scratching with her pen. Then he dozed off and slept the deep sleep of a child until morning.

Next day she was waiting for him outside the school gate. Like all children of poor mothers he was ashamed of her, and pretended at first that he didn't know her. He crossed the street, parted from his companions, and came warily back. She noticed his confusion and didn't take his hand until they were quite alone in the street. They caught the tram to the centre of the town, sitting opposite each other and looking at each other's hands. When they alighted she took his hand again and led him through the rush-hour crowds to Drottningatan. There they stopped in front of a big, grand shop with flashing lights in the window. His mother paused there, and seemed to be reading the window. There was a display of English gramophone records and she read without understanding, and afterwards when they went in she pushed Åke in front of her like a shield.

In grand shops the assistants are always enemies. When you talk to them you turn red, and stammer. 'Can I help you?' they say, as lah-di-dah as if they were speaking a foreign language, and automatically you translate it: 'Can you really afford it?'

Åke's mother said,

'We want to talk into a record. His grandfather's going to be seventy, you see, and he's written a poem to read aloud.'

They had to sit and wait for a time until the recording cubicle was free. The chairs were of cane; they sat on them suspiciously, on the very edge, and whispered. Åke's mother gave him a sheet of paper; it was the poem she had written the night before. He read it, but could make nothing of it. He felt the whole time that the assistants in their smart white coats were staring at him from behind the counter, and he reddened with shame and nervousness. His mother looked about her.

'Don't forget the rhymes,' she said. 'And read aloud.'

He strained his eyes at the paper until they watered. He stared at the rhymes until they echoed inside him: 'Joyful day—all the way; road of life—faithful wife; daily toil—tilled the soil; meadow and ditch—harvest rich; happy meeting—bring our greeting.'

When they were in the hot, cramped cubicle where a woman singer had left a smell of scent, his throat tightened. He gaped, but couldn't get a word out. His mother stood

165

close behind him and held him by the shoulders, and it felt as if she meant to strangle him. Sweat ran down his back in big, warm drops. But when everything was ready and the machine began rasping he managed it somehow; the words loosened and filled his mouth, large and solemn, and the first lines he read out like a priest. When he had finished there was a bit of record left, and his mother bent forward over him and sang 'Long may he live' in her gentle, St Lucy voice.

All that evening she talked about the way he had done it and what a surprise it would be for grandfather and for all the people in the village, for the relations from Uppsala and Gävle, and for the bank-manager and the shopkeeper, when she wound up the gramophone and put on the record. She looked at him, her eyes shone and she clasped her hands under the lamp and sat silent for a long time before beginning all over again.

Next evening she disappeared with a mysterious smile and came back from the neighbour's with a portable gramophone. She set it down in the middle of the table, put the record on as if it were too fragile to be touched, and then gently lowered the needle. They sat under the lamp and listened. At first there was a harsh scraping, and his mother's eyes turned scared and watchful. Then came a panting sound, and Åke reddened, for he recognised it as his own. The voice he could not recognise. He was going to say that the shop had cheated them, but when he glanced up his mother was looking at him with such rapture that he realised the voice must be his. When the song came she tried to look away, but he smiled at her across the gramophone and at last she smiled back.

A little later, after they had switched it off, she said,

'It can't hurt if we listen to it again, can it? The record can stand that much, surely.'

They listened to it again. When they undressed that night she set the gramophone going once more, as if she didn't notice what she was doing. In the middle of the night he woke from a colourful dream. The room was empty, but from the kitchen he heard his own alien voice, and fell asleep again with song in his ears. Next evening they put the record on four times, each time unintentionally, as it were.

One Friday in March at four o'clock they stepped out of the train at the village station. There was a smell of smoke and melting snow. Nobody was there to meet them, but his mother said that that was only natural with all they had to do for the birthday. The road was slippery and long, and Åke wanted to carry the bag, but he wasn't allowed to. But at last his mother had palpitations and was forced to give up, so he was allowed to carry it then, but very carefully. Right at the bottom of it the record lay wrapped in thick newspaper, like a poor woman's only egg.

Nobody was standing on the steps when they arrived. In his father's day somebody would certainly have been waiting there. They walked straight into the kitchen. Grandfather was sitting at the table with a newspaper spread out in front of him, while aunt stood at the stove stirring something in a saucepan. Grandfather looked up from the paper, aunt dropped the spoon.

'Why, here's the widow,' said grandfather. 'What have you got in that bag? Not a present, I'll be bound.'

He went on reading, just as if he'd forgotten that they'd come. The aunt nodded at them and took a fresh grasp of the spoon. They stood abandoned in the middle of the floor and Åke saw his mother's gaze wandering among the copper pans and pot plants. This was the fifth year that she had looked like a widow, black-clad and thin and lonely. Suddenly she looked down at him with a secret joy in her eyes.

'It's a surprise,' she said; but only Åke heard her.

'You might as well start on the dining-room floor,' said aunt, 'and Åke can get out to the woodshed.'

Late that evening she came out to him in the woodshed, put her hand on the hatchet, sat down on the chopping block, and said nothing. She was dressed like a charwoman. She brushed the chips off him. When they were alone she unpacked the bag and stood for a moment under the lamp holding the record tenderly in her hands.

Early in the morning they were up hanging garlands in the big room. The parish clerk and a few farmers looked in and presented grandfather with a walking-stick that had a silver crook handle. They sat in the big room and had coffee and brandy, and at ten o'clock when they'd gone Åke and his mother had to help grandfather over to the sofa.

'What about this surprise of yours?' asked aunt sharply.

'You'll know this evening,' said Åke's mother, winking at her son.

In the evening, relations arrived in cars from Uppsala and Gävle. The long-distance farmers came in yellow spring carts. The bank-manager came and the house was filled with laughter, talk and the smell of cooking. Åke stood in the kitchen peeling potatoes and drying glasses. His mother ran between the big room and the kitchen with food and crockery.

The shopkeeper made a speech and lured them out of the kitchen. They stood in the doorway, listening and looking on. The shopkeeper was already a little drunk and his voice stuck in his throat. With some difficulty he drew a gold watch from his pocket and presented it to the seventy-year-old. Grandfather wept stealthily and a few little tears fell into his brandy glass. The tenant spoke, and also the bank-manager and the relatives from Uppsala and Gävle. Åke's mother poked her son in the side and looked at him meaningly: their moment was coming.

The shopkeeper had brought a gramophone with him; it stood beside the wireless set on the bureau, and without anyone noticing Åke had smuggled the record over to it. When they met in the dark, empty hall, his mother whispered to him,

'Wait until after coffee. I'll give you a nod.'

They drank coffee and brandy, and conviviality was at its height. When Åke's mother had cleared away and Åke went round with cigars and cigarettes, she came and stood in the doorway. He caught her eye and moved cautiously towards the bureau.

Meanwhile aunt was unfolding the card-table. The bank-manager, the shopkeeper, the parish clerk and grandfather took their chairs and sat down round the green table. Åke began to wind up the gramophone. The bank-manager dealt. Mother nodded from the door. The four players picked up their cards, their faces glowing with alcohol and excitement. Åke started the gramophone. Grandfather had a long suit in spades, and he bid first. He was so beside himself with excitement that he dropped his cigar on the floor. Away on the bureau the radio seemed to have started, loudly and irritatingly. It sounded like a lecture. Suddenly he turned to Åke and shouted,

'Can't you turn that damned thing off? Two spades.'

Åke stopped the gramophone. It would make a scratch on the record, but what did that matter? Cold as an eel the pain ran through him. His eyes misted, and the tipsy red faces round him grew as shiny as tin. Somebody from Uppsala or Gävle laughed and the laughter drove him from the room, through the hall and into the darkness of the bedroom. He stood in there with the record in his hands and at last it became as heavy as his own life. The door clicked and in the stream of light his mother came quietly towards him. He slipped into her arms with his pain, and her warm, wet whisperings caressed his cheek.

'Don't cry, son,' she whispered. 'Don't cry.'

But she herself was racked and shaking with her weeping.

TO
KILL
A
CHILD

To Kill a Child

It was a gentle day, and the sun was slanting across the plain. Soon the bells would ring, for it was Sunday. Two children had come upon a path between fields of rye—a path they had never trodden before; and the windows of the three villages of the plain glinted in the sun. Men were shaving before looking-glasses on kitchen tables; women hummed as they sliced bread for breakfast, and children were sitting on the floor buttoning their vests. It was the happy morning of an evil day, for on this day a child was to be killed in the third village, by a happy man. That child was still sitting on the floor buttoning his vest, and the man shaving himself was saying that today they would go for a row down the river, and the woman hummed and put the freshly-cut slices of bread on a blue dish.

No shadow passed over the kitchen, and yet the man who was going to kill the child was standing by a red petrol pump in the first village. He was a happy man. He was looking into the view-finder of a camera, and in it he saw a little blue car and a young girl laughing. While the girl laughed and the man took the lovely picture, the man on the pumps screwed down the cap of the petrol-tank and told them they would have a fine day. The girl got into the car and the man who was going to kill the child took out his wallet and remarked that they were going to drive to the sea, and that there they would hire a boat and row a long, long way out. Through the open windows the girl in the front seat could hear what he said; she shut her eyes, and when she did that she could see the sea and the man beside her in the boat. He wasn't at all a bad man; he was gay and happy, and before getting into the car he stood for a moment in front of the radiator as it glittered in the sun, and enjoyed the brightness of it, and the smell of petrol and bird-cherry. No shadow fell across the car, and the shiny bumper had no dents in it, nor was it red with blood.

But as the man in the car in the first village shut the door on his left and pulled the starter, the woman in the kitchen in the third village opened the cupboard and found that she was out of sugar. The child who had buttoned his vest and tied his shoes was kneeling on the sofa and watching the river as it wound among the alders, and the black skiff drawn up on the grass. The man who was to lose his child had finished shaving and was just folding up the shaving-glass. On the table were coffee-cups, bread, cream and flies. Only sugar was lacking, and the mother told her child to run over to the Larssons' and borrow a few lumps. And as the child opened the door the man called after him to hurry, for the boat was waiting on the bank and they were going to row further than they'd ever rowed before. Running through the garden the child thought all the time about the river and the leaping fish, and no one whispered to him that he had only eight more minutes to live and that the boat would lie where it was all that day and for many days to come.

It wasn't far to the Larssons'—only just over the road—and as the child ran across, the little blue car entered the second village. It was a small village with little red houses and newly-awakened people who sat in their kitchens with their coffee-cups raised, and saw the car dash by on the other side of the hedge followed by a high cloud of dust. The car was travelling very fast, and to the man driving it the poplars and the freshly-tarred telegraph-poles passed dimly by, like shadows. Summer wafted in at the windscreen as they sped out of the village, and steadily and surely they held the crown of the road. They had the road to themselves—then. It was lovely to spin quite alone along a soft, broad road, and out on the plain it was even better. The man was happy and strong, and with his right elbow he could feel the body of his girl. He wasn't at all a bad man. He was in a hurry to get to the sea. He wouldn't have hurt a fly, yet he was just going to kill a child. As they dashed on towards the third village, the girl shut her eyes again and pretended that she wouldn't open them until they could see the sea; and she dreamed—in time to the easy swings of the car—about the brightness of the smooth water.

For life is ordered in so pitiless a fashion that one minute before a happy man kills a child he is still happy, and one minute before a woman screams with horror she may have her eyes shut and be dreaming of the sea, and for the last minute of a child's life the parents of that child may be sitting in the kitchen waiting for sugar, talking about his white teeth and about a trip in a rowing-boat, and the child himself may shut a gate and start to cross a road with a few lumps of sugar wrapped in white paper in his right hand, and see nothing during all this last minute but a long shining river with big fish in it, and a broad skiff with silent oars.

After that everything is too late. After that a blue car stands slewed across the road and a screaming woman takes her hand from her mouth and the hand is bleeding. A man opens the car door and tries to stand on his legs although he has a hole of horror in him. A few white lumps of sugar lie foolishly strewn amid blood and gravel, and a child lies motionless on its stomach with its face pressed hard against the road. After that, two pale people who have not yet drunk their coffee come running out of a gate and see a sight on the road that they will never forget. For it is not true that time heals all wounds. Time does not heal the wounds of a slain child and only very imperfectly heals the pain of a mother who forgot to buy sugar and sent her child across the road to borrow some, and no less imperfectly does it heal the anguish of the once happy man who killed him.

For a man who has killed a child does not drive on down to the sea. He drives slowly home in silence, and beside him sits a mute woman with her hand bandaged, and in all the villages they pass through they see not a single happy person. All the shadows are very dark; and when these two part they are very silent, and the man who killed the child knows that this silence is his enemy, and that he will need years of his life to vanquish it by crying out that it wasn't his fault. But he knows this isn't true, and in his dreams he will wish to have a single minute of his life back, to make that minute different.

But so pitiless is life to him who has killed a child, that afterwards everything is too late.

IN
GRAND-
MOTHER'S
HOUSE

In Grandmother's House

It was quiet in grandmother's house. The little boy stole from room to room; he was looking for the quietness. It must be somewhere. Sitting in a chair, perhaps, rocking, and reading a big book. The boy opened door after door, listening. They were heavy doors; their thresholds were high and shod with gold. He was small and rather frightened, and his heart ticked in his breast like a clock going much too fast. Now he was standing on the last threshold, and there he had to shut his eyes—for who could tell what quietness looked like? He turned his ear to the room to find out whether it was here that quietness was sitting.

He heard a great deal. He heard a great ship rolling along over the sea while the wind howled. And he heard a little girl who couldn't be seen because she was buried under flowers, and she was crying because she was dead. Also he heard grandfather's boots walking to and fro over the wide, creaking floor-boards. But the quietness itself he did not hear, so he opened his eyes and went into the last room.

It was a small room, but in the middle, on the shiny floor, lay a big square of sunlight. The boy stepped into it and stood in it for a long time, listening. It was so quiet in grandmother's house; nothing was stirring in it but his own restless heart. The ship in the picture was still again, and the dead child on the chest of drawers had stopped crying. On the stool in the corner, between the tiled stove and the high window, stood grandfather's tall black boots, and they were silent. Grandfather himself was on the sun now, and when the sun shone grandfather was happy and looked down with kindly eyes. But every time the clouds came grandfather was sad, and he shut himself into his house. When it's raining, the boy thought, it must be hard to be dead.

It was late in the afternoon, and the square of sunlight shrank and shrank, but the boy didn't notice this. He shut his eyes again, and then the strange thing happened: the brightness grew until he himself was filled with light. And suddenly he heard someone whisper: 'Do it now! Now, now!' A clock struck. He crept backwards out of the narrow, shiny strip, and when he opened his eyes he was standing with one of grandfather's heavy boots in his arms. Carefully he set it down on the floor. And the whole world kept silence.

For a thousand years those boots had stood there side by side. They were as old as stone and rock and the path through the woods. Now that they had been suddenly separated from each other there was an inaudible sound, a lament, which seemed to shake the whole room. Quivering in every limb the boy climbed on to the stool and quickly fulfilled his long dream: he lowered himself into the boot, sinking and sinking down the leg of it until he touched the bottom.

There he stood in the boot. Well, and what next? Nothing. He just stood there; the sun went out and softly as a cat the dusk stole into the room. The boy shut his eyes, and as always when he did this something queer happened. This time it was that the boot started walking, with the boy crouching in the leg. It walked straight through the wall into the garden, through the garden, across the road, out on to the bare fields and on over the fens to the dense woods. And wherever it went, noises died. Birds fell silent in the trees, elk paused in the glades with balls of leaves in their mouths and, in the heather, snakes stiffened into black sticks. 'Where are we going?' the boy whispered to the boot, and the boot whispered back, 'We're going to the quietness.' Suddenly a mountain reared its black wall before them, and the boot whispered, 'We go in here.'

But they never did go in, for now came a call that tore open the boy's eyes. It was grandmother. He looked about confusedly in the poky room; he was back and grandmother was calling. It was already dusk and the boot was silent. Grandmother called again and he tried to get out of the boot. Then he found to his alarm that he couldn't: he was stuck. His feet chafed each other in the narrow leg, and the boot enclosed his hips like a stone skin. He wanted to scream, but only his feet screamed, far below him. They were fighting like animals in the dark when an unexpected and frightful thing happened: the boot-leg split and the boy tumbled out on to the floor, and as he crawled there horror stricken, grandmother called for the third time.

With quiet, frozen movements he freed himself. For a little while he stood bolt upright with the split boot in his arms. He shut his eyes as hard as he could, but nothing happened. Inside his eyes there was only a big quiet darkness, and outside his eyes the boot screamed without a sound. It was quiet in grandmother's house, but it was an evil, dangerous quietness. A quietness that was a big wild beast, lurking in the darkness. He had to run away, and to run away he had to commit the final degrading act. He bent down and shoved grandfather's boot deep into the evil darkness under grandmother's bed. Then warily he opened the door of the living-room and prowled in, like a cat.

Grandmother was resting in a chair with a high, high back. The room was dim and the flowers didn't brighten it. Grandmother hadn't lit even the tiniest little lamp. He padded across the rug. Soon he was standing beside her, and she hadn't noticed that he was there. With searching cruelty he scrutinised her white face. Her eyes were closed and he wondered where she was. Perhaps on her way into the bedroom, to look! He caught hold of her arm: she must come away from there. Grandmother cried out and her eyes flew open. He saw at once that she had been somewhere quite different. She shook herself like a dog, smiled at him and said,

'What are you doing, boy?'

'Grandmother,' he asked. 'Where does quietness live?'

A white shell lay on the table before them. He had listened to it many, many times. Grandmother picked it up and pressed it against his ear. It was cold and hard and he wanted to run away.

'What do you hear?' asked grandmother.

'The sea,' he answered.

Oddly enough he was lying. He heard nothing at all. Not the least murmur, and he realised that the shell was dead. He had killed it. Crushed and defiant he laid the shell back on the table.

'No,' said grandmother. 'There isn't any quietness. Everything can be heard. What we call silence is our own deafness. If we weren't so deaf the world wouldn't be so wicked. But luckily there are some people who can hear. There are some who can stand in the plains—do you know what I mean?'

Grandmother was from a country where there were plains.

'Yes,' said the boy. 'Plains are like the fields.'

'Some people can stand in the plains and hear the hills singing. And not only that; they can hear what's happening beyond the hills. They can hear the people who live in the valleys—and even that's not all. They can hear people in the towns struggling and being hurt. They can hear as far as the sea, they hear ships passing at night, and the ringing of the bell-buoys. They can hear farther than that: on the other side

182

of the sea they can hear people screaming when war comes. Do you understand?'

'War,' answered the boy, 'that's soldiers.'

Grandmother was silent, but her words hovered about him like thick smoke. He bent over the table. Beside the shell there was a big yellow astrakhan apple.

'Grandmother,' he asked. 'Can you hear apples too?'

'You can hear anything you like,' answered grandmother. The apple was cold and sour. He pressed it to his ear.

'What can you hear?' asked grandmother.

'I can hear when the wind's blowing,' he said.

But it was a black lie. He heard nothing, and would probably never hear anything again.

'Can *you* hear everything, grandmother?' he asked.

She did not feel his hatred, nor did she answer, but she rose, youthfully and lightly, and took him by the hand. He thought she wanted to go into the bedroom, and fought against it; but they went out. They stood at the top of the steps and looked across the garden where the frosted dahlias were, and apple-trees alight with fruit. There was no wind, and nobody was coming along the road. No bird called and no dog barked in the village. It was quiet, and steeply above them rose the dark blue sky. Stars came out in the clear silence and, further down, a red wall stood up from the earth: the quiet lights of the town shining on the sky.

The boy listened with all his might. He sent his hearing out round the whole earth, and each time it came back empty-handed. But as they stood there in the sparkling quiet at the top of the steps, an apple loosened from a tree and fell upon the hard ground with a clear little thud.

'Did you hear that?' said grandmother, putting an arm round his shoulder as she made ready to speak.

183

'Yes,' said the boy. 'It must be a dog.'

He hadn't heard anything. But grandmother's arm suddenly began to tremble, and at first he couldn't think why.

'Yes,' he went on. 'First a dog's going along the road, and then—and then the soldiers come.'

'The soldiers,' he had said, triumphantly. For all at once he knew why she was trembling. She was afraid. She was afraid because she couldn't hear what he heard. She didn't hear the dog. Perhaps she was more frightened than he was. And he felt that in this superiority lay his salvation. So he continued in his perdition. Grandmother whispered,

'And what comes after the soldiers?'

The boy listened out into the darkness and still heard nothing, not even the hot panting of his fear.

'After the soldiers,' he whispered back, 'after the soldiers there's a heavy waggon.'

'How do you know it's heavy?'

'Because the wheels creak so.'

Grandmother was finding it hard to breathe. A wind passed lingeringly through the trees, but neither of them heard it.

'And what comes after the waggon?'

'A man beating a drum.'

'Why can't I hear the drum?' asked grandmother, almost panting.

'He's beating it very quietly because it's dark,' the boy answered.

A long time passed. 'Perhaps,' the boy thought, icy cold and afraid, 'perhaps she won't ever go indoors again, and if she doesn't go indoors she won't see there's a boot missing.' Grandmother trembled. If there had been anyone who wasn't deaf, that person could have heard grandmother's bones rattling in her body like a rickety old hay-wain. But there

were only deaf people. And out on the road the endless procession moved by in the thickening darkness.

Grandmother whispered,

'What comes after the drum?'.

'After the drum,' said the boy, 'there are two horses.'

'Why can't I hear them?' grandmother complained.

'They've got their hooves muffled because it's dark.'

He felt the evil growing within him like a stone tree.

'And after the horses?'

'After the horses,' answered the boy, 'there's somebody
crying.'

At that moment a bird screeched in the hedge. The boy
heard nothing, but grandmother heard it; and she said,

'I hear, I hear—I'm cold. Let's go in.'

And she hurried in so that she could lock the door against
the evil, but when she looked for the boy he wasn't there.
He realised that all was lost, and shouted as he dashed down
into the garden,

'I'm just going to fetch my ball.'

He had no ball there. He had nothing. But he lay down
at full length under a tree and prayed aloud: 'Dear God,
mend the boot. Dear, dear God let me hear again.' But God
didn't hear him. God simply let the quietness spread itself
like a big, black wing over the boy.

But the stream was still there. It flowed along on the other
side of the road, throwing itself from stone to stone with eager
whispering. He had to go and listen to it, so he sprang up and
dashed to the gate. But he never passed through it, for a man
was coming along the road.

A man was coming through the darkness, and there was
something wrong with him. For one thing, he walked so
queerly. He reeled from ditch to ditch; mostly he was moving

forward, but now and then he went backwards. For another, he sounded so odd. Sometimes he quarrelled with someone who wasn't there, and the next moment he was singing, and when he'd finished singing he quarrelled again. Inside the hedge the boy followed this strange progress with a thumping heart, until the man vanished into the night and was heard no more.

Heard? Yes, he could be heard, but he was only a person, and people can always be heard, because they're there. The boy had to hear something that wasn't there, but he couldn't; and because of that, and because he was cold, he stole indoors.

When he crept into the kitchen grandmother was standing on the threshold of the bedroom, and the moment he saw her face he knew; it had sunk in as if somebody had been digging in it with a spade, and her eyes were staring at him, glazed and big. He realised that she knew everything. And suddenly, without his helping it to come, he screamed at her,

'Grandmother, there's a man lying in the road!'

Bewitched by his lie he saw her coming towards him, trembling and weak. Her mouth moved once or twice, but not a word came from it. As in a dream he saw her poor, trembling arms reaching for the woollen jacket on the peg. Next moment they were out in the darkness. They walked through the dumb garden, and both were trembling. Hand in hand they stepped out on to the black road. It was cold and quiet, and the star-mist quivered above them in space. Suddenly grandmother stopped by the hedge and whispered,

'Where?'

'Not here,' the boy answered. 'Farther on.'

They were walking now in the shadow of the hedge, and the hedge sheltered them, but then it came to an end and grandmother stopped. She dared not go farther, and the boy dared not either—but he had to. A little way on he halted on the gravel by the roadside and bent down.

'Here,' he cried softly.

She didn't follow him, but he heard her say,

'How does he look?'

The boy stared down at the gravel. He picked up a few little stones and answered,

'He's tall. He's awfully big. He's got a hat over his face.'

'Take off the hat,' said grandmother.

The boy raised his hand from the road.

'Is he breathing?' asked grandmother.

The boy turned his head and lowered his ear to the gravel. Lost and desperate he stared with tearless eyes into the deep night. It was quiet throughout the world. A few black trees stood in the meadow like a darkness in the dark; they seemed to him to be moving towards him. He shut his eyes and dropped his head even lower. And just then something extraordinary happened. A current of warm air flowed into the boy's ear. Out of the gravel of the road rose the peaceful breathing of a sleeper.

'Grandmother!' the boy cried joyfully. 'He's asleep! He's asleep!'

From the hedge came a deep sigh.

'Wake him,' said grandmother. 'He mustn't lie out here in the cold like that.'

The boy shook his empty hand in the air. Then he shut his eyes and lowered his ear. From the gravel came a grunting sound and a hoarse whisper.

'What's he saying?' asked grandmother.

'He's saying "You go back indoors—I'm not asleep. I'm just pulling myself together. I'll go on again presently".'

At one jump the boy was back by the hedge. He found

grandmother's hand tucked inside her jersey, and took it, and led her back along the black, safe shadow. Suddenly a fresh wind blew out of the darkness and all the branches began to sway and the leaves rustled. On the other side of the road ran the stream, keeping the stones awake with its whispering, and from the forests of the clouds a strong, serene murmur came down to them.

'Grandmother,' the boy said. 'You needn't be afraid any more. He wasn't dead.'

And his hand felt that she had quite stopped trembling. They went through the garden, the grass rustled and an apple fell. They both heard it.

'Grandmother,' the boy whispered. 'One of grandfather's boots is broken.'

Grandmother said,

'Why, my dear, that doesn't matter. We'll mend it.'

Then in silence they walked up towards the quiet, bright house and a new good night.

A

THOUSAND

YEARS

WITH THE

LORD

A Thousand Years With The Lord

God Visits Newton, 1727

GOD sometimes wearies of manifesting himself in light and silence. Eternity sickens him and his cloak falls. We see a shadow take shape among the stars; the night comes. In Newton's house in London people were unconsciously preparing for the singular visit. Late in the evening a carriage glided along the street through the rain, turned in through the archway and swung round the dark courtyard. The leaves of the oak trees were falling ceaselessly.

Newton's servant got up from the stairs and reeled out into the rain—it was midnight and he was drunk. He saw no coachman and, on closer inspection, no horses. He opened the carriage door: there was no one inside and the seat was cold. On all fours he crawled into the dusty interior and at once fell asleep. The carriage bowled out the way it had come, swerved for a sick dog that was licking the cobblestones, and a little later brushed past a certain lady who was selling herself to Boswell at Tyburn. A sovereign stamped with the head of King George fell to the ground with a tinkle. Boswell laughed and turned up the lady's dress to measure her calf with his graduated cane. Poor Boswell, poor lady! The woman had a wooden leg, hence those trailing skirts. Boswell let his hand slide. God save the falling Night! The lady was wooden throughout. Suddenly snow began falling. Boswell choked, and with his arm round her hard waist he led Miss Gate in among the trees and soon was seen no more.

But the carriage—ah, that passed long ago. The servant snored, snuffled, dreamed . . . yet ever more softly. Fog wreathed the wheels. Dartmoor . . . he was hardly breathing. The servant died, the carriage rolled, soon to be gone for ever.

But God was in Newton's house, on the ground floor. The hall was large and cold. At the farther end a fire was burning on a miserable hearth, and on a stool before it a maidservant had fallen asleep with her head between her broad thighs. Steam rose softly from a cooking-pot. A chilly mouse clambered up the maid's neck and disappeared into her warm hair.

God was now in Newton's study, forty-four stairs above. Here an arrangement existed between Newton of the first part and the outer world of the second part: nobody spoke. For a lifetime Newton had been collecting silence for this mighty room. He had silence from all parts of the world and from many ages too. There was the Ionian silence, the silence between husband and wife, the silence between the dead, the silence over the China Sea, and the Alpine silence. But between two thin silver discs Newton preserved his soul's delight, the climax of his collector's joy: the silence surrounding the torments of Tantalus.

It was midnight, and by the fireplace far behind old Newton, a servant in a red coat was making the midnight tea. With an iron rod he drove off the salamanders that flocked about the trivet. Often the servant wished that he could roar at them as soldiers and maidservants could, but he was born dumb, of dumb parents. Since the beginning of time they had all been dumb—all in his family and the kin of his family. Even his heart was dumb: it beat without a sound. Inanimate objects fell mute under his hand. If this man struck a stone with a hammer, both hammer and stone were silent, and if he approached a braying donkey, the donkey became dumb. He was the son of silence, and Newton loved him.

He placed the steaming tea-pot, the preserves and the

almonds on a silver tray. Then he went to the south-west corner of the room: thirty-six steps. A tall cupboard stood there, of which the upper part disappeared in the darkness among the beams. It was black and the doors were sealed. This was Swedenborg's cupboard, pawned during his last visit to London and unredeemed by him. A cupboard so heavy that six Scots—and drunk at that—had been needed to carry it up to Newton's room. Every midnight the son of silence stooped right down to the foot of the cupboard and pulled out a stiff drawer. In it was a glass bowl with a close-fitting lid. The servant set the bowl on the tray, and with that he was ready to serve his master. Soon Newton would lift the lid of the bowl and with eyes closed inhale Swedenborg's silence. This was a silence unlike any other; it filled him with fear and refreshment of spirit.

But God was in the room, and God's weakness is for miracles. God cannot regard a human situation without transforming it: suffering he transforms into love, love into suffering, dumbness into a voice.

Newton wondered why his servant didn't come. He turned his heavy head away from the blazing candelabras. The servant had halted in the darkness. The tray sparkled, but about his head darkness waved, like tattered banners. Silence had taken wild flight from him; eddies and counter-eddies sprang up in the room and, gripped by a strange unease, Newton rose from his chair.

At this moment the servant dropped the tray. Newton took a step forward, the servant a step back. Then for an eternity both stood motionless, and a singular scene was enacted in the darkness between them. The tray ought to have fallen, but it did not. It remained suspended in the darkness, sparkling and terrible. Then slowly it began rising to the ceiling. And as it rose, tears streamed from Newton's eyes. Tears ran up his forehead like a Niagara of grief. But the servant did not weep; he just stood where he was.

The tray struck the ceiling. Raging and cursing Newton turned, seized a handsome tobacco-pipe and flung it to the floor. But it never reached the floor; it was caught in midflight by the secret criminal who was here transgressing the sacred law of gravity and thrown violently up against the oak beams of the ceiling, where it smashed into a thousand pieces; but those pieces, instead of raining down over Newton, remained suspended in the darkness high above his tearmoistened hair.

Alas, to Newton this was no miracle; it possessed neither the comedy of aberration nor the infinite beauty of the absurd. It was simply and solely a crime, baser and more cruel than all other crimes put together. If he could only have seen the offender—but the criminal hid behind his crimes. Newton pursued him round it, but found him not. During that chase Newton howled, and all the silence that had accumulated in the course of a rare life dispersed now, and fled. At last Newton grasped the mighty cutlass which bloodlessly adorned the chimney-piece and darted at his table, not to stab the servant, who recoiled in horror, but to cut the writing-table itself to pieces—the battlefield of his thought and now the emblem of defeat. The old man raised the weapon with the passion of twenty years, but just as the blow was about to fall, the cutlass by its own motion was torn from his hand; it too rose to the ceiling, to plunge with tremendous force into an oak joist, beside the famous tea-tray.

But as Newton was shaking his fist impotently at the lost instrument of vengeance, the servant freed himself from his position, stepped up to Newton, bowed low and said,

'One moment, Sir, and I will bring it down.'

And in truth: with two flightlike movements of his arms the servant rose into the air. *Mirabile dictu*, he rose magnificently; he was flying. Soon he was up under the ceiling; he bumped his head resoundingly against the oak and then began hauling and tugging at the 'handle' of the sword, as he called it in his uncouth, civilian way. At last he freed it, and saluted his master down there in the brightly illuminated depths. But when their fine eyes met, both men—Newton on the floor and the servant under the ceiling—were struck by the same strange thought, and a more silent silence prevailed. Standing up there in the air about twelve feet above Newton's head, with the cutlass in his left hand and his right quivering with agitation, the servant poured himself a cup of strong tea from Newton's risen tea-pot. He took three great gulps; then, looking respectfully down at his master he cleared his throat and said,

'If I am mistaken, Sir, punish me. If I am right, then order me to be silent. Determine, Sir, whether your servant can speak.'

Then at last Newton understood what was happening: he was witnessing a miracle. And what is a miracle? An exception. And who performs a miracle? God. And who is God? An exception. But what exception? The holy exception: the exception from itself.

And to test the constancy of law Newton now performed an act of which strictly speaking neither his health nor his age allowed. He bent his knees to the very floor and in an attempt to emulate a steel spring he leaped as high as he could. But the servant, who was already pouring out a cup for his master, had to wait for him in vain.

Newton did not fly.

195

He fell heavily back on to his floor, and lying there on the hard boards he began laughing. He laughed till the tears came, and this time the tears ran downwards, down his face. And he got up to preserve the memory of this hour on paper. He seized his quill but could find no ink: it had left the imprisoning ink-pot in a straight, fine jet, and was now to be seen in the form of a huge drop on the sole of the servant's shoe. And Newton could not reach it.

Instead he took a piece of chalk and wrote the following on a blackboard:

A. The nature of human transgression—a dream in the House of Law.

B. The reason for human transgression—despair at not being seen by God.

C. The remedy for human transgression—to be seen by God in the closest proximity.

D. The nature of divine transgression—a vain attempt to replace Law by Miracle.

E. The reason for divine transgression—despair at not reposing in the heart of Creation.

F. The remedy for divine transgression—one day to encounter the eyes of Creation.

(By 'remedy' Newton meant a restoration to health from the crime.)

While Newton was writing the servant mourned, having already discovered the terrible fact about the world of miracles: one is literally exalted above the conditions from which one draws sustenance, one is left with tea and almonds for a fortnight, and then death. Lately dumb, one receives the power to utter one's lament; blind, the power to survey the transgression; paralysed, the grace of running to meet perdition half-way. The servant wept, and soon heavy tear-drops covered Newton's ceiling like crystals.

But Newton had finished. He propped the heavy board against the wall, and above the complaint of his servant he heard the dreadful knocking of a God begging admittance to the House of Law. He signed to his servant to be quiet, but the servant could not refuse the miracle. Newton rose, and with a firm tread left the circle of light about his table, passed the sinking fire and went over to Swedenborg's cupboard. Now he tore the seals from the locks, turned the stiff key and with a sigh of triumph threw open the great doors. And from the empty interior of the cupboard the divine nothingness welled out—the nothingness that fills the oceans between the stars—the pearl of the Universe—holy silence—emptiness blended with light.

The fire flared up, the servant was dumb once more, and not even his heart could be heard. In Newton's room only God's knocking resounded on the door of Creation, with the wail of excluded angels and the hoarse yell of the Flying Dutchman through the tempest.

Newton climbed Swedenborg's cupboard, and from this height beckoned his servant. Beneath the blackened beams the servant came striding through the air with dignity, the tray resting on his outstretched hand. When the man was almost up to him, Newton threw himself off the cupboard and with his arms round his servant's hips, the old man—heavy as the earth itself—drew him down to the floor. Then he led him out of the room, his hands resting like hundred-weights on the man's shoulders—led him downstairs and into the weighing-room next to the kitchen. There Newton filled his pockets with weights, placing in his hands the two heaviest; and these were heavy indeed. Then out on to the steps; it was raining, and everything that had lately happened in that courtyard had long since been rained away.

Newton said to his servant,

'Order a carriage. A Dutch ship has gone aground in the estuary. The captain has swum ashore and is now on his way to London. His clothes are very wet, and it is dark. The captain is cold. Meet him with lights. Bring him here. Don't let go the weights. Don't alight from the carriage. Good night, my friend.'

Newton went up to his room and sat down by the fire to wait. Opposite his chair he placed another waiting chair; then in a second or two he was asleep. A little way behind the place where his servant had come down there was a big ink-splash on the floor, and the night that Newton died and many strangers entered they would marvel at the splash but not understand. And there would be no one to make them understand.

Newton was asleep, but not dreaming. His body was straight and waiting in the upright chair. Suddenly through his sleep he heard rain indoors: rain was falling in his room. He opened his eyes and the fire dazzled him. Heavy drops fell from the ceiling: his servant's tears were obeying the law of gravity once more. Then Newton knew that God had come, and he looked towards the door.

In the darkness by Newton's door God was standing, in the shape of a shipwrecked Dutchman. The tears fell unceasingly and mingled on the floor with the water from the seaman's clothes. God took up his position before the fire and warmed his hands. Taking the tongs, Newton plucked a salamander from the coals and let the creature crawl over the Dutchman's clothes until they were dry.

Then they sat down on the chairs and surveyed one another for a long time in silence. God and Newton.

At two o'clock in the morning Newton said,

'Sire, you are now in Newton's house. Here the law of gravity prevails, which is the love of objects for the earth. Where is my servant?'

'He sleeps,' God answered. 'He sleeps in your carriage.'

'And where is my carriage?'

The Dutchman looked about the room as if seeking it there.

'I see it no longer. It left me. It flew. It rose high over London. But London did not rise.'

'And the horses?'

The sea-captain held out his empty hands. Like an old Jew he showed Newton his salt-roughened palms, and there were no horses.

But Newton was thinking, and while he thought, death drew near. It came in through the gateway and tiptoed past the sleeping maid. Newton drew his watch from his tail-coat pocket and laid it on the floor half-way between the two chairs. It ticked loudly and disturbed their souls' sleep.

At half past two Newton asked,

'What do you seek, Sire?'

God answered, shivering,

'The heart of the world, and my own image.'

Newton pointed to the watch, and he said,

'There is your image, aping you. Just as you circle the dial of the universe in the hope of finding a gap in creation through which you might force your way, so do these hands fly round their own dial, chasing the time they think they measure; but they never find it. I take it that you yourself, in the course of your extensive voyages—most lately on the seas of the world —have realised that the completeness of creation is the corner-stone of misfortunes human and divine. Creator and created —we both suffer in longing for each other, but the longing will never be satisfied. Verily I say unto you: it had been better to create a faulty universe which you might have entered by some secret crack, and so been like one of us, than this creation which for all eternity excludes the creator. I say unto you also: only within Law does peace exist. I am sorry for you, Sire, but time is passing.'

Indeed time was passing very rapidly. The hands of Newton's watch were no longer moving forward at their usual leisurely lope; no, they hurled themselves, howling with fury, round the dial to tear the Roman numerals to pieces, and it was day. The day was grey and their faces grew white. But still the hands increased their speed as if they would smash Newton's watch, and again night fell on London.

'As for my servant,' said Newton, 'he mounted to the ceiling and, although formerly dumb, began to speak. I take it that he is now wandering about the stratosphere drawn by two horses; perhaps he is even singing. Nor do I doubt that high up among the stars, trees are floating—nay, perhaps whole gardens, palaces and cathedrals, armies and navies—which you have released from their contract with the law of gravity. These offences, which by the foolish are called miracles, no more disturb the order of things than the acts of a pickpocket or the misdeeds of a murderer abrogate earthly laws. On the contrary, they strengthen them, for crime always confirms the law; criminals are the confederates of the law, and legislators should send flowers to their funerals.

'But, Sire, miracles in no way diminish the distance from man; on the contrary, they increase it. A miracle wounds the blasphemer and leads the believer to hope in vain, but the heart of the world, Sire, it leaves untouched.'

Now, in this deep night, a carriage could be heard in the street; horses were neighing and someone in London was shouting. The fire died, the candles sank in the candelabras. Both men shifted their chairs nearer to each other. God began to tell of his thousand years on the seas and in Roman cities.

'Often I found my way to other ships. On calm waters my sails were caught by the wind and I was borne forward towards those I longed to take into my arms. A splendid three-master anchored in the sunset; seamen on deck, seamen on the yards—I put the loud-hailer to my mouth to announce my purpose, and my cheeks are tense. Then—then suddenly the masts are clothed in moss, the sails fall to pieces in clouds of dust, the seamen drop to the deck, a frightful stench arises, the planks start and the vessel sinks; and where she sank there stands a tower which sends out lightnings through the night. But when my ship reaches the tower, the tower collapses in rubble and ash, and a shriek mounts above the sea.

'At other times I walk the streets of Roman cities, and a man holds out his hand. I take it, but as I press it the man grows very old; he falls down at my feet. A burial mound grows up over his dust; I lay a flower upon it and, weeping, long to depart. Then I find myself in a house with smooth walls and small windows. In the house are long corridors and many people, and as I pass them they collapse, rot and become earth. The whole house is filled with earth; I find a spade to dig myself out with, but as I seize it the house catches fire. I stand in the sun on a vast plateau covered with ashes, and a man comes towards me holding out his hand. But I don't take it. I rush away, howling like a wolf.'

A light springs up now in Newton's darkness. His watch catches fire, the salamanders creep inquisitively forward.

'Time, Sire, is a terrible mistake. Six days were too many. You should have devoted no more than one to creation, and so rid yourself of a frightful machine. And yet for you, Sire, Time is far more dreadful than it is for man. Man sees only his friend die—he never sees how in that same instant his grave is transformed into a house, the house into a field and the field into a pool of blood. On the mighty dial man can discern one figure only; he does not know that everything has already happened—never dreams that the history of histories, the birth, life and death of the universe, is already accomplished and enclosed in eternity like a ship in a bottle.'

Day again, and the sun glowed over London. The girl slept and the mouse slept in her hair. The vanished carriages pursued their journey. It was growing steadily darker, but steps resounded on the stairs outside Newton's room, voices talked in subdued tones, bells rang and hammers struck. The darkness deepened. Clearly something was happening. Both chairs now moved so close together that soon the question would be: are there two chairs or only one?

But in a voice that caressed God's ear, Newton murmured, 'I believe I have a gift, Sire.'

'What gift?'

'A human life.'

'For what purpose?'

'To be born and to die. For only as a mortal, Sire, will you experience time less as horror than as law. And only within law, Sire, is it possible to touch the heart of the world.'

'Then give me that gift.'

Newton straightened up in his chair, his eyes burning with exaltation. He pulled a bell-rope; there was a ringing everywhere in that great house, and now it appeared that Newton could afford to lose servants, for the doors were thrown open and they entered in a long file: Newton's red-clad servants.

They formed up in a half-circle before their master, who at once began to issue his orders.

To the first he said, 'Fetch a priest!'

And the man threw open a window and called a clergyman who was slinking past the house on his return from a mean adventure.

To the second he said, 'Bring out my dice!'

And he was given dice of ivory and a red bowl to roll them in.

To the third, 'Fetch me all the books you can carry!'

And the third man brought him just that number of books.

To a fourth he called, 'Put wood on the fire and set fresh candles in the candlesticks!'

And this too was done.

But to the fifth he whispered, 'Roll up your sleeves! You're going to fight.'

And the fifth rolled up his sleeves and looked pugnaciously about for his opponent.

God bent his knee by the fire. The priest was led into the room, stinking of strong drink and with his clothes in an evil state, as if he had come direct from the lakes of brimstone.

'Look at this man,' said Newton sternly. 'You are to baptise him. Do you understand?'

He repeated 'Do you understand?' so often and so sternly that at last the priest believed he did understand. His bloated face brightened blissfully; he searched his pockets and felt at his neck for his cross. But the cross had gone, and so with the first finger of his left hand and the middle finger of his right he contrived to form a cross which he held over God's head.

'Open these books,' said Newton to the sixth, seventh and eighth servants, and they did so. In the sixth book was to be read at the top of the open page the word sailmaker, in the seventh the name Claes and in the eighth the name Jensen.

'Throw my dice!'

The ninth servant rolled Newton's dice, and all but the dice were silent: they tumbled and rattled over each other at the bottom of the bowl. The first figure was 24, the second 12, then 18, 6, 7, and 4=71. Newton wrote all this down on a sheet of paper which he handed to the priest. The priest perused the writing and then dropped the paper into the fire.

Then he raised his hands above his head, shaped them to a bowl, and as by a miracle this bowl of flesh and blood was filled to the brim with cool, fresh water. Without spilling a drop the priest poured this water over the strange man's head, reciting clearly and distinctly the following words:

I hereby

baptise thee

Man

as

Sailmaker

Claes Jensen

Born in Newton's Room in London

On the 20th day of March Anno 1727

Or in Bergen, in Norway

On the 24th day of December Anno 1815

Born to lead a Seafarer's Life

To share the hardships of Brothers

And to die a Mortal Death

In Hawaii

On the 7th day of April Anno 1871

Or on Good Friday Hoc Anno.

Then with his still damp hands the priest wiped his sweating forehead, and in so doing received refreshment of a singular kind. He lifted the sailmaker from the floor and kissed him on both cheeks. With that he left Newton's house.

But Newton, seated, said to the sailmaker,

'My friend, you are now a human being and a sailmaker, and ought therefore to be initiated into the condition of a humble man, so that nothing in the life that awaits you may astonish you—neither the actions of others nor your own pain.'

And Newton said to his fifth servant, 'Strike him!'

The servant with the rolled-up sleeves gave the sailmaker two or three hard blows in the face, and the sailmaker received them without a movement. The servant looked at Newton, who with a knitted brow said,

'More fear, my friend! Man's reserves of fear are boundless.' Turning to the servant: 'Spit upon him!'

The servant filled his great mouth with spittle and with a hiss spat into the sailmaker's face. Without a sign the latter wiped his face on his jacket sleeve. But the servant, now on fire with desire to strike and humiliate, gave a howl of rage and was on the point of hurling himself at the sailmaker, when with a look Newton sent him to the rear of the group of servants.

Newton now took a gold coin from his pocket and tossed it carelessly on the floor at the other's feet. When the sailmaker stooped to pick it up, Newton placed his foot upon it and said to the crouching man,

'My friend, learn that attitude by heart. It is called that of humiliation. Kiss my shoe. Then I'll withdraw my foot and the coin is yours—unless I change my mind.'

And what Newton said was done. But when the sailmaker threw the coin into the fire the servants dashed forward and fought with burning arms for the coveted prize. Newton rose from his chair, took his guest by the arm and led him away from the burning servants, out of the room and on to the landing. Newton said,

'I will now show you my house.'

He allowed the sailmaker to pass through a narrow door while he himself stayed outside. The room was narrow and enormously high. In the ceiling was a round hole through which the light poured down. In the wall was another hole, through which darkness poured out. As the sailmaker stood contemplating the dark hole, a great serpent came writhing out of it. The man made for the door, but it was locked. His eyes sought the hole in the ceiling, but the walls were smooth and high and there was no ladder to be seen. The snake rose slowly in close rings; soon it was as tall as the sailmaker and its eyes were on a level with his. He shrieked in horror, but the snake sank again and writhed back into the darkness. The door opened and the sailmaker reeled out into the hall.

'Now you know what fear is,' said Newton, and he led his guest across the hall into another room. This time he came in as well. It was a large, ice-cold room, and on the bare flagstones a negro lay fettered to the ground with heavy iron chains, which cut deep into his flesh. With every pulse-beat a wince of frightful pain ran through the prisoner's frame, and the whites of his eyes flashed like knives in the darkness. The sailmaker asked a gaoler who was bending over the prisoner and gnawing at a big carrot,

'Of what crime is he guilty?' and received the reply,

'Of no crime, Sir.'

The sailmaker snatched the gaoler's bunch of keys and tried them in the locks, but not one of them would fit, and in any case the locks were rusted up. Then he tried to wrench the chains from their fastenings, but they were as inexorably fixed as if they had been riveted to the centre of the earth. The negro, who through his pain had become aware of someone moving beside him, suddenly tossed his head and bit the sailmaker in the shoulder. With tear-blinded eyes the bitten helper groped his way from the room.

Next he entered a drawing-room or music-room, faintly lit by a single candle. At the harpsichord a young woman was sitting. They paused on the threshold, and Newton said gravely,

'My friend, you now know the great human pain which is man's longing to perform a miracle which he has no power to perform. Now you shall learn the greatest human pain of all: the perception of the impossibility of love.'

With these words Newton left the room, but the sailmaker walked on tiptoe to the harpsichord, and as he approached it the woman began to play. She played so entrancingly that he was compelled to fall on his knees at her feet. And in the light of the one candle he saw a face of such entrancing beauty that at first he was seized with reverence for the unknown lady, then with love for her and lastly with desire for her. And when he laid his hand on her warm arm and asked her to go with him, she rested her white hands like snow on the keys, looked at him so gently, sorrowfully and lovingly that his soul swooned, and answered in a low voice,

'I will stay with you for a thousand years.'

At this blissful moment the door was flung open and in dashed some kind of workmen. Laughingly and noisily they hurried up to the harpsichord, tore the hair off the sailmaker's beloved and threw it into a big hamper. They twisted the beloved's head round and round like a screw until it came off, and the sailmaker saw that it had indeed been screwed into a torso of iron. The arms went the same way, and the hands were unscrewed from the wrists—everything vanished into that insatiable hamper. The men hurried out as gaily as they had come in, swinging the hamper between them like a big cradle.

But the sailmaker felt a light touch on his shoulder, and started out of his pain. Newton was standing behind him.

'My friend, you loved a doll.'

'But she played for me.'

'Your love believed so.'

'But her eyes looked upon me with human brilliance, and her arm was as warm as yours, sir.'

'Your love believed so.'

'But she spoke to me, sir, and promised me a thousand years.'

'Your love believed so.'

They went out of the room, the candle was extinguished behind them and the lid of the harpsichord fell. They walked downstairs into the big, cold hall, where the sleeping maid sat before her fire and her cooking-pot.

'Are you hungry?'

At once the sailmaker felt a fearful hunger raging in his body. He nodded, and Newton nudged the girl so that she tumbled off her stool. She sprang up, yelling with fury. Newton calmed her with a look.

'Give this beggar some food!'

The maid took a bowl from the floor, and this bowl was so dirty that neither bottom nor sides could be seen. Yet she turned it over, emptied out the flies into the cooking-pot, grasped a ladle and began ladling out the beggar's supper into the loathsome bowl. Meanwhile Newton and the sailmaker stepped forward and looked down into the pot. They saw a big rat floating in the stinking brew, and with every spoonful the girl pushed it out of the way. At the bottom of the pot they saw some big stones, some of which were caught up and ladled into the bowl. Then the maid handed the bowl to the sailmaker with so careless a movement that half the stew splashed over his feet; he put the bowl to his lips and emptied it, except for the stones. Then he gave it back to the maid, who blew her nose into the stew, sank back on her stool and fell into a deep sleep; and the little mouse, which had been observing the scene from the top of her head, fell asleep too.

But Newton said to the sailmaker, whose hunger was now appeased,

'Do not rely on man's generosity, but learn to love the food of beggars.'

Steps were heard on the stairs. A servant in a half-burnt livery, with a sooty face, came hurrying towards them. His eyes were sly and mercenary, and he held Newton's coin, rescued from the fire, tightly in the crease of his thumb.

'Sir, you are waited for,' he shouted, and dropped the coin, which rolled through the archway into the street with the man after it.

Newton looked about him in his house. He was pale, and his eyes sank deep into his head like stones. He stood on the bottom stair, turned towards his guest and said in a barely audible voice,

'Already we must part, then. This is indeed sad—*très triste. Enfin.* . . .'

He climbed another two stairs and then, appearing to change his mind, walked slowly down again towards the sailmaker, who was waiting motionless beside the snoring maid. Newton moved close up to his friend, so close that in the gathering darkness one could not have said whether one or two people were standing at the foot of the stairs. Looking intently into the other's eyes he said softly,

'Sire, I will give you another miracle.'

Newton's face was suddenly overspread with a red glow as of fire, and pressing his mouth to the sailmaker's ear he seemed to whisper something. The sailmaker nodded very gravely several times, and then at last they parted. This time Newton did not look back. Swiftly but without undue haste he mounted the long staircase, while the sailmaker stood and watched him until his eyes were blurred. When clarity returned, the empty stairway soared up before him, but Newton he saw no more.

The servant walked past whistling, tossing his coin and catching it. The maid snored, the mouse in her hair snored, and under the cooking-pot the fire was beginning to die down. A beggar slunk in from the street, sniffing his way towards the stew, like a dog. With pleasure he saw the sailmaker disappearing up the stairs, and the soundly sleeping maid; he lifted the pot noiselessly from the fire, then vanished triumphantly with his booty.

But the sailmaker's steps were heavy, and the frightful cold that now penetrated the house froze his blood. Reluctantly he pressed down the ice-cold door-handle and stepped into Newton's room. He was surprised to find so many people already assembled. There were not only servants in that great circle. Relatives, hastily aroused in the middle of the night, were standing in carelessly-donned wigs, holding their little hands in the air. There were doctors, discussing, measuring and brandishing shining instruments; and a group of men whom he recognised as fashionable theologians were turning the pages of books, now and then raising their pale hands towards the ceiling. They were all gathered about Newton, who was dead.

Newton lay dead in the middle of the room—but more than that. Newton lay dead in the *middle* of the room, between floor and ceiling. Peacefully the great Newton reposed about three feet in the air. And his relations said,

'How shall we explain this to the world? Alas, what will our own order say to it? The peers, the Court. . . . Dear God what a scandal. Can no one get that man down on to the floor?'

Some actually made a few feeble attempts, but these were doomed to failure. They pressed Newton's body lightly with gloved hands, with little result. Newton lay where he lay, and the doctors said,

'This is impossible, unwholesome and scandalous. This is a physical aberration, a gross deception and a scientific enormity. Newton is going too far. He has always wanted to outdo us simpler souls—but really this is going too far.'

They felt Newton, they pinched him, they opened him up here and there; but this concerned Newton not at all. He lay where he lay, and the physicians who put their ears to his body to listen for escaping gas heard nothing, for there was no gas. Then the physicians, very despondent, placed their instrument-cases and medicine-chests on the body to weigh it down; but the great Newton bore such trivial burdens with ease, and the theologians said, as they added to these burdens with their writings,

'This is ungodliness. This is Devil's Divinity. This is indeed sin. So far as we know, not even Queen Cleopatra of Egypt, Herod Agrippa, the Persecutor or Nero who burned Rome, refused to descend to earth after their death.'

Then they took their books from Newton's body and looked through them, but to their sorrow they found no precedent for the ungodly act of hovering between heaven and earth when dead. But the most eager careerist among them composed at once, at Newton's writing-table, the draft of a paper to be submitted to an extraordinary Church Convocation, declaring that corpses floating in the air ought not to repose in consecrated ground, and suggesting the propriety of a debate upon whether or no the air surrounding such remains might be consecrated.

Meanwhile the secretary of the Medical Society was taking accurate measurements of Newton's elevation from the floor, movement imparted to the body by the passing to and fro of relatives, and other like matters, and was just calculating Newton's gravity-constant with the aid of theological works and writing-cases placed upon the body, when an appalling clashing and clanking disturbed the peace of living and dead.

Two sooty smiths appeared in the doorway, dragging between them an enormously massive chain of great length. They had been sent for by one of Newton's relatives, an army officer from the Highlands, who had already foreseen the ruin of his career and who in the face of this prospect had hatched the first and only idea of his life. Those present made room for the blacksmiths; and these, without any marked respect for the dead man, who was unknown to them, wrapped him up in their black chain. They swathed great Newton as if he were a child, from ankles to neck, and when they had finished he sank heavily to the floor, to the relief of the mourners. Only the secretary of the Medical Society left in a huff; and the pushing theologian, enraged, tore up his draft with his teeth.

But all the rest gathered round Newton's vanquished body, shed tears over him, recited prayers and made signs. The writing-cases disappeared, incense was kindled, books were slipped into clerical pockets, wigs were straightened and the fetters hidden under a pall of black silk; for now it was day, and the peers of England, French counts and German barons were already stepping from their coaches to pay a last *visite d'honneur*.

Now the coffin, quickly! The carpenters struck their final blows and galloped into Newton's room with his last bed. They had set down the beautiful coffin on the floor and stepped reverently aside when the crowd uttered a cry of dismay. *The coffin had risen to Newton's former level and was now impossible to budge.* Everybody shouted at once, wigs slipped askew, and the Highland major called for more blacksmiths.

Blacksmiths came from all over London. Roughly they jostled aside the velvet-clad assembly in front of Newton's gate and climbed bent-kneed up the stairs with their thunderous burden, while peers, counts and barons stood still, stricken dumb at these singular attendants. On reaching Newton's room the blacksmiths filled Newton's coffin almost to the brim with the heaviest chains in London—and once more brute weight triumphed over feather-light miracle. At last the chain-clad Newton was placed in his chain-filled coffin, and not by a sign did he betray the least discomfiture.

More candles, larger tears, more incense, fewer physicians, fewer theologians, more bishops. In with the archbishops! Out with the blacksmiths! Admit the dukes! The great Newton awaits you. *Allons, comtesses*, bitte *die Baronen*! Newton *vous attend. Und die Tränen fallen aus dem edlen Baum.* Newton smiled for the last time and the coffin was shut. But forcing his way out through the brilliant throng went the sailmaker Claes Jensen who, for the benefit of his future existence, had incorporated the image of the floating Newton with his immortal soul.

Outside Newton's house he was a stranger, and he asked a poor boy the way to the port of London, for he was born a seafarer. The boy pointed in some direction or other and the sailmaker set off accordingly, but before long became involved in a mighty throng. A huge funeral procession was moving up the broad street and he enquired of the bystanders—all women —who was being taken to his grave. A hundred astonished faces were turned up to his, and he saw that all the prostitutes in London were garlanding the stately cortège; that they were all weeping and that their tears had ploughed deep furrows in their paint. And a hoarse voice whispered in his ear,

'Great Boswell is being buried today.'

And as the splendid hearse passed the prostitutes they wept and lifted their skirts above their thighs, and round their thighs they were wearing black garters. But the sailmaker too wept at this sight, for the first time he observed in others a disinterested sorrow, and deeply moved he disappeared into London's alleys.

But now came the fog, and the town which was already a stranger now became a star without light; the sailmaker had to grope his way forward, yet with the seafarer so strong in him that he took the straightest way to the port of London. Suddenly he was again in a throng, far worse than the other, and through the fog he dimly glimpsed a mighty procession resembling a line of smoothly gliding ships, with lofty stems and sterns and broad decks. And above the procession the fog was white with screaming gulls; now and then guns were fired close by his ear and he shouted over the crowd,

'Who is this who is being carried to his grave?'

And with one thunderous voice the people of all London answered through the advancing fog,

'Great Nelson is being buried today.'

Then the sailmaker knew that he was on the right road, and he plunged so deep into the densest darkness that no one saw any more of him. And with him went all sounds. Only the sky dripped and dripped, and his steps dripped between the hidden houses.

When he had gone quite a long way towards the sea he was met by the wind, and the fog lifted. And suddenly, as by magic the fog rose straight into the sky. The sun shone hard and gloriously. He walked along a newly-tarred jetty and in towards a town. The gables shone at him in shimmering colours, the windows sparkled, a white horse lifted its muzzle from a crate of herring and neighed as he passed by. Leaning against this merry horse he took off his heavy shoes, and when that was done he flung them out into the blue water, where they sank at once.

Softly snow began to fall. The sun went out. Stars were lit. The moon rose. Barefoot the sailmaker continued his walk to Bergen, in the land of Norway.